A SIMPLE SUBURBAN MURDER

Michael Denneny, General Editor

Stonewall Inn Editions

Buddies by Ethan Mordden
Joseph and the Old Man by Christopher Davis
Blackbird by Larry Duplechan
Gay Priest by Malcolm Boyd
Privates by Gene Horowitz
Taking Care of Mrs. Carroll by Paul Monette
Conversations with My Elders by Boze Hadleigh
Epidemic of Courage by Lon Nungesser
One Last Waltz by Ethan Mordden
Gay Spirit by Mark Thompson
As If After Sex by Joseph Torchia
The Mayor of Castro Street by Randy Shilts
Nocturnes for the King of Naples by Edmund White
Alienated Affections by Seymour Kleinberg
Sunday's Child by Edward Phillips
The God of Ecstasy by Arthur Evans
Valley of the Shadow by Christopher Davis
Love Alone by Paul Monette
The Boys and Their Baby by Larry Wolff
On Being Gay by Brian McNaught
Parisian Lives by Samuel M. Steward
Living the Spirit by Will Roscoe, ed.
Everybody Loves You by Ethan Mordden
Untold Decades by Robert Patrick
Gay and Lesbian Poetry in Our Time by Carl Morse and Joan Larkin, eds.
Reports from the holocaust: the making of an AIDS activist
    by Larry Kramer

Stonewall Inn Mysteries

Death Takes the Stage by Donald Ward
Sherlock Holmes and the Mysterious Friend of Oscar Wilde
    by Russell A. Brown
A Simple Suburban Murder by Mark Richard Zubro

A Simple Suburban Murder

Mark Richard Zubro

ST. MARTIN'S PRESS
NEW YORK

Design by Holly Block

Library of Congress Cataloging-in-Publication Data

Zubro, Mark Richard.
  A simple surburban murder.
    I. Title.
PS3576.U225S5 1989   813'.54   88-29864
ISBN 0-312-02640-4
ISBN 0-312-03933-6 (pbk)

10 9 8 7 6 5

For Kathy

I unlocked my classroom door and stepped inside. I stopped. Someone sat in the last desk in the last row farthest from the door. The window blind was down and in the early-morning dimness I couldn't tell who it was.

I flipped on the lights. "Hello, good morning," I called. There was no response. With the light on I could tell it was a male. He didn't move. Whoever it was had his head cradled in his arms on the desktop, face turned away from the door.

What the hell was someone doing here? I dropped my briefcase on top of my desk, tossed my overcoat after it, and started down the aisle. Halfway to the desk I recognized Jim Evans, the math teacher. I glanced at my watch: 6:53. Jim Evans never showed up early for school. He always walked in at 7:35, precisely on time for work, usually the last one here.

I reached him, called his name, touched his shoulder. The body was cold. He was dead.

I shuddered briefly. I'd seen death before, when I was a marine in Vietnam. It never got easier to deal with, but I'd learned to accept the reality.

I walked to the intercom button, pressed it.

"Yes, Mr. Mason." It was Georgette Constantine, the school secretary.

"Would you send Mr. Sylvester to my classroom, Georgette, and call the police?"

"Mr. Sylvester is busy, Mr. Mason." She paused. "You want me to call whom?"

"The police, Georgette."

"Really, Mr. Mason, I can't do that. Mr. Sylvester has to make that kind of decision."

"Georgette, whatever Sylvester is doing—"

She interrupted, "He's with parents now, Mr. Mason. You know I'm not to disturb him when he's with parents. He always tells me parent-school relationships are the most important."

I was not up to mustering the patience it normally took to deal with her. I said, "Georgette, listen, you will call the police. Tell them there's a dead person in my classroom."

"What?" Her voice squeaked.

"A dead body, Georgette. After you call the police you are to go to Mr. Sylvester's office, interrupt him, and tell him what I told you."

"Mr. Mason." She sounded faint.

"Do it now, Georgette." I switched off the intercom.

I walked back to Jim Evans. Carefully I checked the body. There was no obvious wound. Then I raised the head. Jim Evans was no longer a handsome man. Someone had caved in the whole left side of his face. Blood caked on his head and the arms of his coat.

Among the 150 or so teachers in the district he was barely an acquaintance, not a friend. Our paths seldom crossed. Why was he dead, and why was his body in my classroom?

‹ 2 ›

The desks sat in neat rows, books rested in proper order on the shelves. There was no blunt instrument covered with blood and gore. I checked the top of the desk and the floor for bloodstains. A little, but not much. He'd been killed somewhere else and brought here.

I heard the door open. Alfred Sylvester walked in. Compared to him, Ichabod Crane would look robust. He was in his early sixties and almost completely bald.

I stood between him and the corpse.

"What's the meaning of this? How dare you order my secretary around? I'm not to be disturbed."

I moved so he could see the corpse. I pointed to it. He shut up.

"Jim Evans is dead," I said.

"How can that be?" He inched closer to the body. Five feet away he stopped. His face turned white. "Why does this have to happen to me?" He moaned. Abruptly he sat down in the desk closest to him.

"It happened to Evans," I reminded him.

He talked on as if he hadn't heard me. "There's no sub for his classes. He didn't call in saying he'd be out today. Who could I get this late? This is some sick joke."

There was a commotion in the doorway. Crammed there were four kids from my remedial English class who came in early each morning for help with their work. The first, Jill Anderson, took a step inside the door.

"Mr. Mason?" Her voice was tentative.

Her words sparked Sylvester to life. "You kids get out of here. You don't belong here now." He rushed over to them, shooing them out the door.

Sporadic mumbles of "What's going on? What is this?" broke out from them, but they moved. He slammed the door on them and turned to me. "We can't let the kids know about this. They'll never be able to handle it, and their parents! What are the parents going to say? They'll blame me.

I'll have to call the superintendent." He bounced on his toes as he talked, his thin body jerking spasmodically.

I walked slowly up to him and spoke softly. "We need to call his family; his wife needs to know. The kids at school will find out eventually. It's best if they're told up front and honestly. We also need to—"

He snapped, "I know what we need to do. I can handle this. There's going to be trouble."

The door swung open. The police walked in.

I teach remedial sophomores and honors seniors English at Grover Cleveland High School in River's Edge, a far southwest suburb of Chicago. The school is over fifty years old. The roof leaks when it rains.

I've been teaching since leaving the marines. I guess I'm odd. I still love teaching after fourteen years. The money's never going to make me rich, but I wouldn't trade the joy of seeing a child learn for anything.

My boss, Alfred Sylvester, is a major-league asshole. If there was a World Series for idiot administrators, he'd be most valuable player—unanimously. I watched him fawn at the police, blithering out various inanities.

Early on I perched myself on my desk out of the way.

The first two cops examined the body quickly. They were young guys. From their tentativeness I guessed this was probably their first murder, maybe even their first time with violent death. One left to get help. The other hung around looking lost. He asked me my name and if I was the one who found the body.

I answered the two questions.

He wandered toward the corpse, stopped halfway between it and me, and stood aimlessly.

In a short while the room began to fill with official-looking people. They talked to Sylvester and got him out of the room.

The detective who seemed to be in charge finally came over to me. He introduced himself. "I'm Detective John Robertson."

"Tom Mason." I shook his hand.

"You found the body?"

"Yes."

"Want to tell me about it?"

I told him the story.

When I finished he asked, "Are you sure the door was locked?"

"Yes, I had to use my key."

"Who else has a key?"

"I'm not sure. Lots of different people have used this room over the years. I doubt if they've kept accurate records. Besides, some of the keys to the other classrooms open this one too. These locks are easy to break into. Teachers forget their keys all the time. It would take a janitor half a day to get here to open it. Some of us have broken in ourselves. A few let the kids do it for them."

"Terrific." He sounded disgusted. "We'll have to check everybody's keys anyway. Probably useless. The murderer might have had the sense to throw it away."

Since the doors had a spring lock it wasn't odd that I had to use the key to get in. They put in spring locks years ago because teachers kept forgetting to lock their doors, and kids got in and took unnailed-down materials.

Robertson gave me a suspicious look. I kept silent. He was in his early thirties, dark haired, gray suited, with a gray overcoat frayed at the cuffs. He looked like his kids, job, wife, or mistress—or all four—wore him to a frazzle.

"Did you kill him?" he asked abruptly.

I expected the question. I returned his piercing look. "No," I said.

Frank Murphy walked in. He was a police detective I knew

well. We'd worked together with numerous troubled teen-agers and their families for many years. Even after he was transferred to homocide we kept in touch.

Robertson explained the situation. Murphy told him we'd worked together before, that I'd been helpful to the police in dealing with troubled kids.

Robertson shrugged, accepted the statement, and turned to the matter at hand. "What's the story on Evans? What was he like?" he asked me.

"I didn't know him well," I answered. "I saw him maybe once or twice a year at teacher's meetings, but I barely knew him to talk to. I had his oldest boy as a sophomore two years ago."

"What's his wife like?"

I thought a moment. "I only met her once. I remember a small plump woman, grayish and faded, worried about the kids. She didn't know what to do about the oldest boy, Phil, the one I had at the time. She said she couldn't control him. I listened, tried to give her a few suggestions. I think mine was the only class he passed that year. She was grateful for that."

"Isn't it odd that a teacher's kid would be flunking?" Robertson asked.

I gave him a grim smile. "Not really. Teachers have the same problems with their kids that any other parent does. Sometimes I think teachers with kids who aren't making it in school are more defensive."

"Was Evans?"

"I never talked to him about his kid."

"Why not?"

"Like I said, the boy passed my class. He never gave me a hassle. It was the mom who had the problem at home."

"Anything else you know about the wife or family?"

"Nothing about Mrs. Evans. I think there are several

younger kids. One might be in eighth grade this year. If I'm not mistaken there are two younger girls."

"How about the kid, Phil? What was mom worried about?"

"That was two years ago. It's tough to remember. As I said, I picture her as anxious, worried. Sorry I can't be more specific."

Murphy asked, "What about the other kids at school? What did they think of Evans as a teacher?"

"They complained about him a lot, but then kids complain about most teachers. But there were some who thought he was great."

"What was the big complaint?"

"The usual, too much homework, graded too tough. He made every kid do these massive projects every year. It would count for a whole quarter grade. The slow kids could barely read the math book, much less do the projects. They also claimed he played favorites. Maybe he did. The brighter kids were the ones who tended to like him. A few said he was the best teacher they ever had." Most teachers do what we can to avoid favorites. Some kids are more likable than others. Some are jerks. You try to be fair. Some teachers are more successful at it than others.

"Any kids you know with grudges, active dislikes, enough to kill?"

I shook my head. "Not that I've heard. In fact, this year the kids have said very little about him at all."

"How about the faculty, any enemies there, any major quarrels?"

"Not that I know of. You've got to realize that with over 150 faculty members, we see very few people other than those in our own department."

There was a momentary pause. Robertson shifted his

weight from one foot to the other. Finally he asked, "Where were you last night, Mr. Mason?"

I understood that since I found the body I was a suspect. "I spent the evening home alone. I had no visitors or phone calls."

It was after eleven o'clock by the time they finished with me. I stopped in the school office to find out where my class was.

In the office Georgette fluttered nervously at the teachers' mailboxes, cramming memos into them. She gasped when she saw me. "Aren't you going home?" she said. "I'd need a sedative. If I came in and found"—she gulped—"found what you did. I'd be a nervous wreck. You should sit down for a while. Do you want to lie down? There's a couch in the nurse's office. Or can I get you something?"

"No, thank you, Georgette. Do you know where my class is meeting?"

"No, I don't. I think Mr. Sylvester knows." She gave another little gasp. "I just remembered." She clutched her throat, lowered her voice to a whisper, and said, "They want to meet with you."

"Who does?"

"Mr. Sylvester and the superintendent. He called earlier. I had the hardest time finding Mr. Sylvester."

Long ago I ceased being impressed with principals and superintendents. "Do they want to see me now, Georgette?"

"I'll buzz Mr. Sylvester." She spoke into the intercom on her desk then looked up at me. "They'll see you now, Mr. Mason."

I walked to the door of Sylvester's office.

"Mr. Mason," Georgette called. I turned back to her. "Do the police, did they"—she hesitated over the words—"do they know who did it?"

"No, Georgette."

"Do you think someone from school did this?"

"I don't know."

She glanced fearfully at the office door as if a gang of murderers might rush in any moment to claim her as their next victim.

Row upon row of rigidly straight plaques filled with platitudes covered one entire wall of Sylvester's office. The other walls were barren. The desk, chairs, computer, filing cabinets, and carpet were all various shades of gray. The lone window looked out on the faculty parking lot.

The superintendent stood in the center of this uniformity. Jason Brompton Armstrong took up a major portion of what was not a small office. Blimp was a rude but accurate word for him. He wore a black suit and a red tie. His head was bald on top with a gray fringe around the sides. His manner said salesman with all the negative connotations attached to that word and profession. He gave me a big smile, spread his arms in friendly welcome. This made him look like a blimp ready to land. I mistrusted the look in his eyes, his smile, and the way he stood.

We exchanged greetings. Sylvester flopped officiously behind his desk. He looked fawning and alert. Armstrong subsided his bulk onto the metallic couch. I was not invited to sit. I did so anyway. The superintendent spoke. "Mr. Mason, can I call you Tom?" He didn't pause for a response. "I asked to meet with you this morning. Mr. Sylvester was kind enough to arrange it."

Arrange what? I walked into the office. Georgette told me about a meeting. Of course, arranging meetings of such simplicity was about Sylvester's level of ability.

"We wanted to be sure you were all right."

"I'm fine, thanks." What the hell did they want?

"Well, good, good. I wanted to be sure. You don't need a

few days off? We'd be happy to give it to you. It must have been quite a shock walking in on, well, quite a shock."

"A little out of the ordinary," I admitted.

He laughed uproariously. Sylvester echoed him. Armstrong chortled and slapped his knee. "You're a cool customer, Tom."

"Thanks for the offer," I said, "but I'm fine."

He gave me a searching look. "Well, that's good, that's great. I checked your file before I came, all top ratings. A good, good teacher. That's great. And I saw that you were a marine. That's what I like. We've got to be tough, don't we? Strength is our only defense."

I watched his unfriendly fat as he prattled non sequiturs. The end-of-class bell rang. We all looked at our watches. "Well, time's rushing," Armstrong said, "I'll get to the point. I think the thing to remember is that in unfortunate situations such as this the most important thing is to minimize the risk of the school district being seen in a bad light in the community. We don't want them to think we aren't in control. We don't want any more bad publicity. It's bad enough as it is, all three TV networks here filming, the district's name linked to murder on TV, terrible, terrible, and a man dead of course, horribly sad. I wish I'd known him." He paused to look sad and then quickly continued. "But now the important thing is to remain dignified and serene. We have to be above all this awful mess. Don't you agree?"

It sounded like pure bullshit to me. I simply looked at him.

Sylvester answered for me. "I'm sure Tom agrees that we don't want any unfortunate slips to jeopardize our position, our standing in the community."

Armstrong frowned him to silence. "Tom, we would prefer if this wasn't discussed with the students, or other faculty members, and when you talk to the police, if you remember that the district has been good to you for fourteen years. Police can be hardheaded. We must be seen in a good light, and of course if reporters ask you anything, you'll refer them to us."

I didn't like what he said, and I resented his nerve in saying it. Plus the whole thing was suspicious as hell. What were these two up to? I rethought my acidic response. I gave them a neutral promise. "I'll do what I can."

I wanted a chance to sort out what these two were up to. Maybe I'm too suspicious of administrators. All of them I've dealt with lie, some less than others. Few are actually outright evil human beings. These two were putting on some kind of show and I wanted to know why. I tried to look sincere and benign. The tardy bell rang. It was time for the next class to begin. Briefly Armstrong looked suspicious, but he shrugged it away.

*   *   *

The group of seniors I tutor after school arrived on time, a rarity. The four of them, Lee Jones, Alice Delderfield, Greg Davis, and Paul Howard, clustered around my desk.

"You're all a little early today," I commented.

"We want to know what happened," Lee blurted out. He played right defensive tackle on the football team. The knocks to his head hadn't added anything to his performance in school. They couldn't possibly have hurt either, unfortunately.

Alice said, "What was it like, Mr. Mason?" Alice was a pleasantly ditzy girl.

Briefly I explained what happened.

"How awful!" was Alice's reaction.

"Was there a lot of blood?" Lee asked. He attended every blood-and-guts, machine-gun-them-all movie that came out.

"Don't be gross," Alice said.

He rolled his eyes, gave her a disgusted look. "Girls don't

understand anything. Mr. Mason can handle this stuff. He was in the marines in Vietnam." Besides being a teenage sexist pig, he also thinks my being in the marines qualifies me as second to God. This I learned from his parole officer, who also suggested I never disabuse the boy of this notion, since I was the first teacher in five years the kid did any schoolwork for.

I said, "I don't think telling all the gruesome details would be helpful, and don't be sexist, Lee."

Greg broke in. "You know the creepiest part is that it happened in school." Recently Greg had grown a mustache. It leant him a certain rakish air. Alice had informed me that all the girls thought it made him very sexy.

"This whole thing is creepy," Alice said.

"Especially Mr. Evans," Lee said.

"What an awful thing to say," Alice told him. "You aren't supposed to say mean things about dead people."

"I don't care," Lee said to her, then turned to me. "Mr. Mason, you said it's always better to be honest."

My curiosity was up. I said, "I haven't heard you talk about him this year. What brought on these negative feelings? You didn't have him this year, did you?"

"No," Lee replied, "I had him last year. I tell you he was creepy to be around."

"How so, creepy?" I asked.

"Well, there were always rumors about him." Lee looked at the others. For one of the rare times since I'd known him he hesitated.

Alice goaded him on. "You're so brave, talking about honest, go ahead tell him. I dare you."

I saw Greg give Lee a warning look.

Lee was caught now. His nemesis, Alice, pushing him to speak, but his buddy, Greg, pulling him to silence.

Paul, the quiet one in the bunch, broke the logjam.

"What the heck? What's the big deal?" He shrugged his boney shoulders. "It was all kids' talk."

"What was?" I asked.

Paul broke the circle around the desk and began hunting through the pile for his after-school work. We were in the science room. I'd stacked their work on a nearby table. He talked with his back to us. "They said he gave the bright senior girls A's if they would have sex with him."

"Paul!" Alice shrieked.

"Alice, please lower your decibels," I said.

Paul took his materials to a desk. He looked up at us. "What's the big deal?" His voice was flat, almost bored. "There's no proof that he ever did it. I think a bunch of kids who didn't like him made it up. Kids make up all kinds of stuff." He folded his lanky frame into a desk, turned to his work, and proceeded to ignore us.

Lee puffed his chest out and throwing caution aside, said, "I know it's true. I heard once—"

"Hold it, Lee," I interrupted. "We don't need more rumors. Before you say anything be sure you have proof for it."

"Well, I don't have proof, but everybody says—"

"Not 'everybody says,' Lee. Something you saw with your own eyes."

He looked sullen. "I didn't actually see him, but—"

"No buts."

Lee looked disgusted. "All right, but come on, Mr. Mason, you said you wanted to know stuff." A new thought struck him. "Are you going to be a detective and solve the murder? We all could help."

"Slow down, Lee. The police are taking care of the murder investigation. I only asked because you knew him better than I did, and you expressed some negative feelings."

"You mean I'm a suspect?" He sounded almost hopeful.

"No such luck."

He was crestfallen. "I can't even be a suspect. You won't listen to what I have to say." His tone was more depressed than angry. "Stupid proof." Then his face brightened. "At least I do have proof about his kid, that Phil Evans."

I thought I knew Phil pretty well, but I wanted to learn as much about the Evans family as I could, including the kids.

Alice piped up, "He's probably just going to tell you that Phil ran around with a bunch of kids who wrecked stuff and stole things when they were in eighth grade."

"Was not," Lee objected.

Alice ignored him. "Everybody knows it already." She sneered.

"I didn't," I said.

"What I know nobody else knows," Lee boasted.

"What's that?" I asked.

Lee didn't look to the others for approval this time. "He's a faggot. Last year I saw him and another guy in Lincoln Park in Chicago. He and this other guy were kissing."

"Oh, gross," Alice said.

"Come on, Lee, are you sure it was him?" I said.

"I was as close to him then as I am to you now."

"Didn't he recognize you?"

"Nah, he was too busy kissing, ugh."

Alice broke in, "What were you doing there?"

Lee looked sheepish. "I took a girl to the zoo." This was extremely uncharacteristic, non-macho behavior on Lee's part. He growled, "I only took her there because she insisted we go. It was a cheap date."

"I think it's sweet," Alice said.

He gave her a dirty look, then went back to his story. "I saw him as we walked through the park to get to the zoo."

Lee didn't sound like he made the story up. I had another thought. "Did you recognize who he was with?"

"Never saw the other guy before. He was real old, like you, Mr. Mason."

"I don't consider thirty-eight old."

"Oh, sorry, you know what I mean—an adult, an old guy."

"This was last year, when he was a junior?" I asked.

"Last summer," Lee said.

I looked at the others for confirmation. Greg rallied to Lee's support. "I heard rumors about him too. Lots of kids think he's gay. I don't think he is." He pointed at Lee accusingly. "You never told me about this." The two of them were good friends.

"It was summer. You weren't around, and I forgot about it until now."

"Yeah, you forgot, you don't remember nothing half the time," Greg said.

"Anything," I corrected.

Alice turned up her nose. "I think this whole discussion is icky. I won't talk about those kind of people. The whole family is so sad. I think they should be left alone."

Teenage reticence took over. Discussion drifted into more mundane topics.

An hour later the kids left and I went in search of Meg Swarthmore, our ancient and learned librarian, and ultimate clearing house for all school gossip. If there were secrets to be known, Meg would have them to tell.

She perched in her usual spot on a tall stool behind the book return: a tiny woman, not much over five feet tall, and plump in a grandmotherly way.

"Hi, sexy" was her greeting. "You're in here so rarely these days I figured I better cut the bull and get to what interests me. So how about a hot date?"

I glanced around checking for kids.

She laughed when she saw me. She teased, "You mean

you didn't plan this visit, waiting until all the kids were gone to come in and ravish me?" She twisted her kindly face into a brief pout, then a wicked grin, and finally gave a melodramatic sigh. "But you're too young for me and already spoken for."

I smiled contentedly.

"I admire you, Tom. Thirty-eight years old, settled down, living in unmarried bliss with a gorgeous blond. My kids and even grandkids—there's no respect these days—keep trying to fix me up with these creaky old coots. Most of them belong in an iron lung, or do they still have those things in this day and age?"

"I don't know."

"No matter. I used to believe in true love and happiness forever."

Her husband left her thirty-five years ago with three kids to raise. He never came back. I gave her the same answer I always did. "Maybe someday, Meg."

"I've turned down enough men to start a small country of my own." She laughed. "Whoever he is he'll have to do a hell of a lot better than the others."

I smiled at her. "The three of us will go out to dinner soon."

"Great. I'll look forward to it." She held my gaze for several moments. She patted my hand. "You're still in love. I wish you both the best of luck. You of all the people I know deserve true love and happiness." She took a deep breath, and then continued briskly. "Okay, you want the lowdown on Jim Evans."

"You read minds now, Meg?"

"This one wasn't hard. I barely see you for ages. You find somebody murdered in your classroom. You'd have to be a dunce not to be curious about what the hell he was doing there, and who killed him. So of course being a normal person, you'd want to find out more. And where's the best place to find out? Me, of course. I've been expecting you." She gave a furtive look around. "It's still a couple minutes until closing, but I'd rather talk in total privacy in my office."

She hopped off her chair, went to the library door, and took a quick survey of the hall. "Sylvester's been lurking around lately near closing time," she explained. "Maybe he thinks I'm stealing his precious books. I've taken to bringing large bulky purses just to drive him nuts."

I like Meg.

We walked into her office and settled ourselves onto either end of a cozy little couch.

"Are you coping okay with what's happened?" she asked.

"Yeah, I think I'm all right. It'll hit me more later when there isn't as much activity."

"Police, kids, and Sylvester running around all day makes for a lot of hectic," Meg said.

She sighed. "You want to know about Evans. Let's start with the basics: married for twenty years, four kids—two boys, seventeen and thirteen, two girls, ten and eight, taught here twenty-one years, his first job out of college. Marriage has been rocky. There was talk of divorce five or six years ago. It blew over though. They worked out some compromises. He agreed to joint marriage counseling. She agreed to separate vacations once a year. One goes while the other stays with the kids. That sounds strange to me, but in this day and age, who knows? Another part of the agreement is that neither asks questions of the other when they get back."

"Unbelievable."

"Belief is a chancy business, I've found."

"That's true. So what else has our less-than-model husband been up to?"

"He also wasn't much of a model father. A large part of the problem was abuse."

"His wife?"

Meg shook her head. "The kids."

"That creep," I echoed my students. "All of his kids?"

"Supposedly he concentrated on the older boy, hurting him significantly at times."

"And nothing was done?"

"You know how it is, Tom. He was never violent enough to put the kid in the hospital, and even then you see parents get away with it time after time. When they are caught with clear proof, getting the system to work in the kid's favor is a rarity."

"I never knew this when I had Phil in class."

"It's not something people are likely to talk about, especially kids. Besides, I presume his stopping the abuse was part of the agreement back those five or six years."

"Do you know if he really did stop?"

"As far as I've heard, yes."

"What about his wife? Why didn't she leave him?"

"Facts first—she's two years younger than her husband, pretty once, now looks ten years older than she is. No education beyond high school, always involved with P.T.A. and room mothers. Why didn't she leave? Who knows? Love, lack of alternatives, fear. It could be any number of things."

"Would she want to kill him?"

"You'd have to ask her that."

I thought for a minute. "How about the family's financial situation?"

"Sometimes he had tons of money. Threw it around all over the place. Other times he was flat broke. Supposedly one time he tried to pawn one of his kid's baseball uniforms."

"What caused the swings?"

"That I don't know."

"That's a hell of a way for a family to live," I commented.

"Real sad," Meg replied.

"What about at school, Meg? The kids today hinted about him trading grades for sexual favors from the senior girls."

"I very much doubt it. I've heard the rumor. I've never been able to confirm it." Her voice got angry, showing the tough woman underneath. "But if I found out he was, the bastard would've been out on his ass and in jail, and I'd have been the one to throw him there." Her voice returned to normal. "But as I said, no confirmation on that one, and my sources are the best in the school. That doesn't mean he wasn't doing it. My sources are great but not omniscient."

"How'd he get along with the faculty?"

"For some talking to him was like being beaten to death with an all-day sucker. I thought it was phony. To others, especially secretaries in the math department, he was incredibly cruel."

"Any particular enemies in the department itself?"

"Definitely yes, although I can't give you names. The department is intensely competitive. You've met Leonard Vance, the department head?"

I nodded.

"The man is brilliant but slightly nuts. He's the only faculty member who's been here longer than me."

"Is that the part that makes him nuts?"

She smiled, brushed aside my crack with a wave of her hand. "No, he's harmless enough. He's been divorced twenty years. He's been asking me out for the past ten. I always turn him down. He isn't my type. As for the department, he's got them tuned to an incredible pitch. The competitiveness comes from him. Over the years he's gotten a lot of work out of his staff and the kids. At what cost I'm not sure."

"So, the math department is not heaven on earth," I said.

"You can say that if you want. What's important is I don't think you'll find your murderer there. They're an academically competitive group, but as personalities I'd mark them in the wimp category."

"Then who did it, Meg?"

"While my sources are good, catching murderers is not in their job description."

"How reliable is your information?"

"It's better than gossip or rumor. Is it absolute truth? I don't know if such a thing exists. Is it factual? I think so. I do know the last time I steered somebody wrong was over seventeen years ago."

"Are you going to volunteer this information to the police?"

"Are you sure you were in the marines? I never volunteer, honey. If they want to talk to an old gossip they can come to me. I suspect they'll find out most of this information without me."

I thought over what she'd said. "One other thing," I asked. "What about the older boy? Do you know anything about him? The kids said he might be gay."

"There I can't help you. I keep a strictly adult grapevine. Long ago I decided to let kids be themselves. They have their world. We adults have enough problems in our own."

I rose to leave. "Well, thanks, Meg. You've been a big help."

"Say hello to Scott for me."

"I will," I said and left.

I realized my briefcase and overcoat were still in my classroom. The school was cold and quiet. The windows were dark. My footsteps echoed on the wooden floors in the dimly lit halls. At my classroom door I paused over the police seal. It was nothing but a piece of ribbon loosely stretched across the doorway. I opened the door, stooped under the ribbon, and walked in. I didn't bother to turn on the lights; the soft glow from the hall was sufficient for me to make my way to the desk. I glanced to where the body had been. There were only mute desks resting for the next day's onslaught. I picked up my things and turned toward the door.

A shadow in back of the room moved. I turned toward it. "Who's there?" I said.

There was a flash and a roar. The briefcase burst out of my hand.

I dove to the floor and scrambled behind the desk. I heard the outer door slam. Seconds later another shot split the night. Glass shattered. I waited. Silence ticked by. I felt the breeze from the hole in the window. I raised my head slightly to try to get a view outside. I couldn't see anything. Then I heard footsteps, people hurrying. A minute later a small group clustered in the doorway.

"Tom?" It was Meg, her voice edged with fear.

"I'm here, Meg. Don't turn—" Before I could say it the lights flashed on. I saw Sylvester with his hand on the switch. He stooped under the police ribbon and entered the room. He presented a fantastic target for anyone still outside. Stupidity can kill, but in this case the victim survived. Maybe they realized how useless it would be to shoot only one administrator.

"Will someone turn off the lights," I hissed from behind the desk.

Meg responded, edging carefully around Sylvester to the light switch. She turned them off. "Are you all right?" she asked.

"Yeah," I said. I crawled over to the window, reached up carefully, and lowered the blinds. Then I stood up and brushed myself off. I turned the lights back on. All the desk and file cabinet drawers gaped wide open. Large drifts of the contents cascaded around the back of the room.

"What are you doing in here?" Sylvester demanded. "And what was that noise?" Several of the night custodians moved into the room behind Sylvester.

I examined the tattered remnants of my briefcase.

"We'll have to call the police. The window will have to be boarded up," Sylvester complained, "and look at this mess. More trouble. I'll never get out of here tonight."

I examined the damage. The shot had passed through the briefcase and blown off a section of the top corner of the desk. I'd turned the correct direction at the right instant, or maybe whoever fired had poor aim, or the darkness was too much of a hindrance. For the first time since I found the body I felt fear. My room hardly qualified as simply being the next convenient place the killer came to for dropping a body. Now Sylvester's question wasn't so dumb. Why me?

Scott said the same basic thing later that night. I lay on my stomach on the couch in blue jeans and white gym socks. He was similarly clad, perched on top of me, massaging my back.

He's the only one who has that perfect touch, between a caress, tickle, and massage, that is pure bliss. I hadn't been able to get hold of him all day. His heavy and erratic schedule of speaking engagements often left us only the brief minutes before bed in which to talk. When he got to my place, I'd told him of the events of the day.

"So what did the police say the second time?" he asked.

"Not much. There was no one around outside by the time

they arrived. No one saw anything, so there was nothing they could do. They wrote it off as random vandalism against the school. They didn't seem terribly concerned."

"Well, I am," he grumbled in his deep voice.

I shifted my weight slightly. He gets heavy, but I love the backrubs. He's six four, well muscled, without an ounce of fat on him.

"I found a flashlight the intruder dropped. It wasn't random violence. I think it's connected to the murder. But what could I have that the person who murdered Evans could want? That's what I've been thinking the past few hours." I shook my head. "I don't know what I'm in the middle of."

"Danger," he said.

"Yeah, that, and murder, but why? I barely even knew Evans." His fingers kneaded my lower back. "I'm going to keep trying to find out what I can. There must be some connection."

"I'd like to help," Scott offered.

"Thanks," I said.

"And the first thing I think I should do is move in with you until this is settled."

Scott's been campaigning to move in for several years. Meg's right, I do love him, but cohabitation might be difficult. One reason is he's extremely closeted. Being a professional baseball player makes it harder for him, of course, but he keeps his orientation and my existence desperate secrets. He hasn't told anyone in his family, or any of his friends or teammates. I don't care to live that way. We spend a lot of holidays with my family. His family is in Georgia and doesn't know about us, he visits them once a year without me. My father and brothers get puffed up with pride having a star baseball player in the house. My nieces and nephews love him. Last Christmas he spent hours rolling around outside in the snow with them. At least once each visit my mother and sister corner me in the kitchen to tell me how wonderful he is and then say that we should live together. I fend them off.

"Lift up," I said. I felt his weight ease. I flipped onto my back. He sat back down. I looked up at him. "Until this is settled it might be a good idea," I conceded.

"And I should put in that alarm system."

He's been trying to get me to install a security system. He's hideously mechanical. I have seen him lay his hands over a crippled machine and the damn thing heals. I think they're afraid of him. They know he means business. He could put in an alarm system easily enough. Until that moment I'd always thought it was silly for me to have one. Now I wasn't sure. I told him I'd give it serious consideration.

He leaned down and kissed me. I reached back and switched off the lamp. I put my arms around him and pulled him close.

The next morning he cooked breakfast while I got ready for school. Over breakfast we talked options.

"I'm going to cancel my schedule today," he said.

"Don't," I said, "there's no need. There's not much to do. I'll be safe at school."

He gave me an exasperated look. "You weren't yesterday."

"You can't stand guard in my classroom all day."

"I want to at least drive you to school and pick you up."

"It's only a ten-minute ride. Besides, someone might recognize you."

"I don't want you hurt," he said.

"Okay, you can drop me off. I'll get a ride home from Meg."

"And I'll pick you up." He stopped my protest. "My schedule is light today. I'll do some rearranging and be there."

At noon I went to talk to Leonard Vance, head of the math department. I wanted to talk to people and find out more about the man found dead in my room. Vance was in the math department office.

He was in his late sixties. He wore baggy pants that clung under his potbelly, only partially concealed by a fraying sweater. I explained what I wanted. We went into his private office to talk. The room had a battered old desk and two rickety chairs, none of which matched.

After we sat down Vance said, "I don't know how much I can help or even tell you. I've already talked to the police."

To break through his reluctance I said, "I know you don't know me, but as I said, I'm trying to find out more about Evans. Maybe it's curiosity, a lot of it's because I found the body. It's just I want to know, to understand. I'm not interested in secrets so much as finding out about Evans as a person."

He rubbed his chin. "You're a friend of Meg's. She and I haven't always seen eye to eye, but she's a solid person. We've worked together a long time. She talks about you. Says you do a good job with slow kids. She admires you a lot." He paused. "I'll give it a try."

He thought a minute more then said, "If I had to use one word to describe Jim Evans, it would be competitive. He always had to be the first, the best, with the most. You may have heard that the department puts a premium on excellence."

I nodded.

"But he took it to extremes. He'd fight viciously at every faculty meeting on every topic, even down to who got the most paper clips. He always needed to win. If he ever lost a vote in the department, the office here turned into a living hell. He lost as often as he won."

"How would he show his anger?"

"With a constant barrage of vicious remarks, sniping at everyone. More than once he's brought a new teacher or secretary to tears with something he said. Evans was good at making enemies. Sure we're competitive, but not to the vicious level Evans was. But that wasn't the worst. You might wonder why I didn't report him to the administration. The answer is simple. They were good friends. Evans used to run to Sylvester to snitch on teachers. You know the type of fighting and bickering that goes on."

"You couldn't report him, and at times he'd be undercutting your authority?" I said.

"Say we were considering a curriculum change that he didn't like. If he thought the vote would go against him, he'd run to that clown Sylvester, to try to get that jerk to be on his side, so Sylvester would force us to do what Evans wanted."

"Did he ever succeed at that?"

"Not really, but he caused enormous headaches because of it. The key, as you probably know, with Sylvester is twofold. One, he can be successfully menaced, as all would be bullies can. And two, whoever talks to him last gets the favorable decision. If Evans was crossed he wouldn't try to solve the problem. He'd just keep braying like the jackass he was. He was fairly good at fighting, but he wasn't any good at politics, and at that I am a master."

"Are you sure it was him snitching?"

He smiled. "I trapped him several times. I gave him information, told him the other faculty knew, but not to discuss it yet. The information was bogus. I'd told no one else. Sylvester invariably called me in to discuss what I told Evans within half a day after I told the little snitch."

"Did you ever confront him?"

"Yes. He denied it all, even after I told him he was the only one that I gave the information to. He outright lied to me."

"He sounds like a miserable person to work with."

"He was. In his defense I must say that I didn't personally

dislike him. He could be expansive and friendly. Plus I pride myself on being able to say that I can work with anyone."

I thought a minute, tried another tack. "Did he have any special enemies? Any one person he feuded with most often?"

"You'd have to line up the whole math department, and it wouldn't be a question of which ones were his enemies, but who could come up with the most reasons for disliking him."

"But Sylvester must have thought he was the greatest."

"Presumably. Besides his spy reports, Evans was always down there kissing ass with Sylvester, and Armstrong too, for that matter."

"Wait a second," I said. "This morning Armstrong claimed he never met Evans."

"He's lying. I saw them together at least two or three times."

"Can you remember when this was?"

"It was quite late after the last few department meetings. One time I heard the three of them talking in the inner office. The door wasn't tightly closed. And once I saw the three of them walking out of the office. They were distant from me, but you can't mistake the Blimp."

"The time you heard their voices, are you sure it was them?"

"Oh, yes. We department heads meet with the superintendent at least once a month. He drones on in that endlessly cheerful way, so I'm used to his voice. Sylvester and Evans I would recognize in the normal course of events."

"Could you tell what they were saying?"

He thought a moment. "No, I can't help you there."

After he picked me up, Scott and I spent an hour working out at my place. I live in a farmhouse in the middle of one of the last cornfields in southwestern Cook County. The subdivisions creep closer every year. Soon I'll want to sell. I own the house and two acres around it. I like the quiet. The fields belong to a farmer I've only seen at a distance as he works the land.

Scott and I agree that working out together is one of our biggest turnons. I can still wear the same size gym shorts I wore when I played sports in high school. We work out in gym shoes, white socks, old running shorts, and much-used jock straps. Many times the workout has been interrupted for more intimate activities. We work out together as often as we can.

That evening we went to the funeral home. Often when going out, Scott's fear of being recognized limits us. Several times in restaurants we've had to leave before finishing because of persistent and obnoxious fans. Other times we've been in the most public of places and no one has said a thing. It's not so much being seen with another male and people thinking he's gay, but to keep away from the admiring hordes. At a gathering such as this I doubted there would be much trouble.

The funeral home was crowded. Amid the strangers, I recognized several faculty members and parents.

I spotted Mrs. Evans and went up to her. She looked tired and subdued.

"I'm so sorry," I said.

"Mr. Mason, thank you for coming." She turned a pasty white. "You're the one who found him."

"Yes."

"It's so awful." She glanced up at me tearfully. "I remember when you had Phil in class. You tried to help. I could tell you cared. I don't know what I would have done if it hadn't been for you. You were wonderful."

"I hope I helped," was all I could think of to say.

Abruptly she seemed to come to some decision. She glanced quickly around and lowered her voice to a whisper.

"I must talk to you." She took my arm and led me down a corridor to a private room. She closed the door and stood in the middle of the floor, trembling.

"What is it, Mrs. Evans?" I went to her, put my hand on her arm.

"I'm glad he's dead," she snarled. "He was an evil and cruel man."

I didn't know what to say.

She continued. "He abused all of us, hurting the children, bullying me. I feel like I'm waking up from a hideous nightmare. I can't tell them out there." She jerked her head toward the door. "They'd never understand the dutiful wife who hated every breath the bastard took." She began crying.

"It's all right," I said, patting her arm awkwardly.

"I'm not crying for him." Her voice was fierce. "I want you to know that. It's like I'm on a roller coaster. One minute I'm so happy he's gone, and the next I realize I have nothing to fall back on. I've never had a job. I have no skills. I have no idea what's going to happen to the children and me."

She stepped away from me, found a Kleenex in her purse, and dabbed at her eyes. "I didn't kill him," she said. "I couldn't. I'm not strong enough, although there were a thousand times I wish I had been, but I didn't kill him."

She put the Kleenex back in her purse, stood up straighter. "I didn't ask you here to slobber all over you. You've got to help me. Phil is missing. I'm worried."

"Missing? For how long?"

"Since yesterday. He talked to the police around two o'clock at the house. He left around four and never came back. I didn't hear anything during the night. This morning he wasn't at breakfast. I checked his room. The bed was perfectly made. There was no note. He hasn't been back all day. I called the school, but he didn't show up there either."

"Have you told the police?"

"No, I'm afraid to. They'll think he had some part in killing his father. I know they will. He's a good boy, moody, like so many teenagers are, but a good son."

"Maybe he's simply off grieving by himself?"

She gave a short laugh. "They hated each other. Jim used to beat Phil when he was younger. The last time Jim tried, a couple years ago, he didn't realize how much Phil had grown up. The boy fought back. I thought they would kill each other. And I'm afraid Phil knows things about his father."

"What makes you think that?"

"There were times, not that long ago, when Phil would talk to me, but not for a while now. He hasn't talked to anyone at home for months. When we did speak, I'd urge him to talk to his father. I wanted them to get along. I wanted us to be a normal family. But Phil refused. He'd say to me, 'Mom, don't pressure me to talk with Dad, or to talk about him.' The way he said it frightened me. It's as if he knew things that a child shouldn't know. I didn't dare press him for more."

"Did he ever threaten his father?"

"The time I told you about, when they fought, at the end, before running out of the house, Phil screamed at his dad, 'If you ever touch me again I'll kill you.' But I know he didn't mean it, Mr. Mason. He was angry. I made him apologize for that later."

"Did he?"

"Yes, I begged him to, for me." She gave me a forlorn look. "I wish he would come home."

"Has he ever left before?"

"Sometimes he's stayed out late, but he's never been gone overnight without telling me."

"Do you know who he might stay with?"

"No, we have no relatives here."

"How about his friends? Who are they?"

"None of his old friends called recently. I think he cut himself off from them. I know he used to be friends with Greg Davis, but he hasn't mentioned Greg in months."

"He must be somewhere, Mrs. Evans, probably with some friend close by. Did he have any money, a savings account to draw on?"

"No savings, but he's had a lot of money lately. I asked him where he got it. He wouldn't tell me."

"Was he dealing drugs?"

She gave me a fearful look. "I don't know. What do I do? You've got to help me, Mr. Mason."

"I will if I can, but I think you should tell the police. They'll find out he's missing sooner or later. They have resources for finding someone."

"I can't, not yet anyway. I just want him to come home."

"I'll try to talk to some of the kids at school," I said. "I doubt if I can do much, but I'll do what I can."

"Oh, thank you, Mr. Mason. Thank you."

I found Scott waiting in the viewing room. In the short hallway leading outside I told him about my conversation with Mrs. Evans. "Her intensity at times worries me; she might be close to a breakdown."

"Poor woman," Scott said, "but there probably isn't a lot we can do."

"That's true," I said. "The police will find out Phil is missing soon enough. Still, I'm going to check it out."

We left. From where we parked you could see down the alley behind the funeral home. As we neared the car I noticed a lone figure in the alley sitting on a stack of tires. I pointed him out to Scott. "I think that's the Evans boy, the eighth grader. I remember he used to wait for his brother after school when Phil was in my tutoring group. I think his name is Keith. Let's talk to him."

The boy looked up briefly as we approached. He wore a suit and tie with no overcoat. He shivered in the chill November night.

"Cold to be out tonight, son," I said.

He peered up at me. "Who are you?" His voice was petulant.

"Tom Mason. You're Keith Evans, aren't you? Phil's brother? I was his teacher."

"Oh, yeah," he said without enthusiasm.

"It's a little cold to be out without an overcoat."

He shrugged.

I sat down on the stack of tires next to him. He looked at me. For the first time he glanced at Scott. His eyes got very wide. "You're Scott Carpenter," he exclaimed.

"I am." Scott sat down on the other side of him.

"I know you," Keith said. "You came and talked at our sports banquet last year. You're cool."

"Thank you," Scott said. "I'm also cold. Why don't we go inside?"

"Not in there with all those people," Keith said.

I suggested the fast-food restaurant across from the funeral home as an alternative. Keith agreed. Scott and I had coffee. Keith wolfed down enormous quantities of food. He had his dad's handsome face, with his hair longer than the fashion.

"This is great," he said. He pointed to the massed food in front of him. "Whenever we go out with my family we can only order the least expensive thing on the menu."

"How come you weren't inside?" I asked.

"I couldn't stand all those adults slobbering over me. So I walked out." He stopped eating and stared wistfully across the street to the funeral home. He spoke softly. "I wanted to see where they put my dad." His voice grew softer. "I wanted to see what he looked like."

"You didn't get a chance?" I asked equally as quietly.

He shook his head. "There were too many people around. I was waiting for everybody to leave."

We sat in silence for a while. He finished the last of his French fries.

"Want any more?" I asked.

"No, thanks. I'm stuffed, Mr. Mason."

Throughout the conversation he'd been stealing glances at Scott. Now he said, "I want to be a baseball player like you, Mr. Carpenter, when I grow up."

"I hope you make it," Scott said.

"I play all the sports at school—baseball, football, everything." He was an average-size kid, maybe a little bigger. Hardly the type for football, I thought. But with his suit coat folded behind him, his white shirt couldn't conceal the broadening of teenage shoulders and hints of a lithe muscularity.

He continued. "I can't believe I'm sitting here with Scott Carpenter. The other kids will never believe this."

"It's true," Scott said.

Keith got a confused look on his face. "Did you know my dad?"

"No, I'm a friend of Tom's. I came with him."

"Keith, do you know that Phil is gone?" I asked.

He lowered his head, mumbled an answer.

"Keith," Scott said.

The boy looked at his hero.

Scott said, "If you know anything about where he is, you should tell us."

Keith looked torn. "I promised," he said finally.

"It's important for us to know. He might need our help," Scott said.

There was silence. The kid looked miserable.

"He told you he was leaving," I prompted.

Keith nodded.

"Is he coming back?" I continued.

A negative shake of the head.

"Is he in the Chicago area?"

"I don't know. I think so. He said he'd call me."

"Did he leave because of what happened to your dad?"

Now there was fear in the boy's eyes. "I don't know," he said.

"Did he murder your dad?"

"No," he whispered.

"They used to fight a lot, didn't they?" I asked.

"Yeah, sometimes it was horrible."

"What did they fight about?"

"Everything. We all hid when they fought, including my mom. It used to scare me when I was little."

"And now?"

"Usually I leave the house, go over to a friend's and stay."

"Did you and your dad ever fight, Keith?" I asked.

His no came too quickly.

"Did your dad ever hurt you, Keith?"

"No." He wouldn't meet my eyes. "He didn't, really. My dad was okay."

Scott said, "If he hurt you, Keith, it's okay to tell us."

The boy sat with his eyes lowered. I looked at Keith. I tried a few other questions about his dad, but he wouldn't talk about him. Keith was like many kids with an abusive parent.

They covered up for the parent and wouldn't admit anything. I gave up and went back to Phil's leaving.

"Did Phil say when he'd call?" I asked.

"No, just that he'd call soon. And that I would go live with him. He said he could make enough money for us to live on. He said that adults only ever messed things up." He looked from one to the other of us.

We talked for fifteen more minutes. The boy gave no further information. He still wanted to see his dad, so we took him across the street to the funeral home. Mrs. Evans looked startled when she saw him. I explained the situation to her. She seemed more upset and torn.

"I want to see him, Mom," Keith said.

"But the casket is closed," she objected.

"I want to," he insisted.

With what looked like an heroic effort, she pulled herself together, took him by the hand. "All right" was all she said. Together they walked to the casket.

In the car on the way home Scott said, "I don't understand Keith."

"What don't you understand?"

"He seemed to be acting almost normal. Protecting his brother rang true. But I don't know, I expected him to be more broken up about his dad's death."

"He must have a lot of strong ambiguous feelings about his dad, if what the mother told me is true. With a home like that you can't blame the kid for reacting strangely."

"I guess you're right. You know, I bet the kid knows a lot more than he's saying about where Phil is."

"I agree. I think his brother told him a lot more than Keith told us tonight."

"Do you think Phil or Keith might have killed their dad?" Scott asked.

"I thought of that. I don't know about Phil. I haven't really talked to him in two years. I want to talk to him. As for Keith, I doubt it. He doesn't seem big enough."

"Maybe he had help," Scott suggested.

"Or maybe he helped his brother," I said. "We need to find Phil."

"For what it's worth," Scott said, "I don't think Keith did it."

"Yeah, my suspicions are with Phil and the adults. Mrs. Evans sounds like a great suspect. I bet the police think so too. She couldn't hide that much hate from them. They'd find out from the neighbors, if nowhere else."

"From what you say she's too much of a mouse to have done it."

"At times, but pushed to the edge, who knows what she might be capable of?"

"That's true. Who else?"

"I don't trust Sylvester and Armstrong."

Scott looked surprised. "Not trusting them is one thing. Linking them to murder sounds a bit of a stretch to me."

"Those two are up to something. Maybe they were in cahoots with Evans, mixed up with him, something. They acted awfully suspicious to me. And more important, they'd have access to the school, something neither Mrs. Evans nor her kids would have. I'm not ready to accuse them of murder, but I'd bet money they've gone beyond simple administrative incompetence."

"You're prejudiced," Scott said.

"I guess." I pulled into the driveway and turned off the car. "This leaves out people we don't know. We have no idea what Evans's life was like outside of school. Hell, I've only talked to Vance in the math department, although I trust him pretty much. I've got people to talk to tomorrow."

       *   *   *

At noon the next day I started with the school social

worker. I hoped she'd give me more background on the Evans family. What Nancy Lacey said was "I'm sorry, that information is confidential. I am not at liberty to discuss the situation." Her November tan was from the same place she got a size-4 figure, a health club. She was twenty-four years old and gorgeous. This was her first job after college.

I explained my reasons for inquiring.

"You're wasting your time. All records, conversations, any dealings with students through this office cannot be discussed with outsiders."

She'd early on caught the disease of many school social workers. Its basic symptom—don't trust the teachers.

"Aren't we supposed to be working together to help children?" I asked.

"I don't think you understand how the guidance and counseling office works." Her tone was that of those who condescend to the poor stupid teachers—you don't have counseling degrees so you don't know how to handle kids.

I cut her off. "Save your condescension for someone who will put up with it."

"Mr. Sylvester has given me strict instructions. I intend to follow them. I want you to leave my office now."

"What instructions from Sylvester?" I asked.

She clamped her mouth closed, stood up, and pointed to the door.

I left. She probably would report me to Sylvester. I could expect a visit from him before the day was over.

During the tutoring session after school I talked to Greg. I got right to the point. "Greg, several people have told me that you're a good friend of Phil Evans."

"Well, yeah, sort of," he said. He shifted uncomfortably.

"Did you know that he's missing?"

He shook his head. "I didn't know that."

"It's true. I'm trying to find him. Do you know where he might have gone?"

"Look, Mr. Mason, you've got to understand about me and Phil. We were buddies for years. I've known him since first grade, but like, I don't want you to think that maybe I, you know, like what Lee said yesterday."

"That you and he were friends, but you never had anything to do with him sexually."

"Right."

"You seemed surprised yesterday when Lee told. Did you know Phil was gay?"

"Not really. I only heard rumors this school year. I kind of stayed away from him when I started to hear them. I didn't want people to start talking about me too. I started hanging out with a new crowd."

"Before you drifted apart, did he ever talk about running away?"

"Sure, yeah, all the time, because of all the hassles he had with his dad."

"Did he say where he might go?"

"He always talked about going to California and getting a job in a rock band. We went to all the big concerts together when they came to Chicago."

"If he wanted to stay somewhere closer for a while, which friends would he go to?"

"I was it. He was a loner."

"When you guys used to hang around together, did you go anyplace special, or did he mention anyplace he might stay? Anything that gives you an idea where he might be hanging out?"

He thought a moment, then spoke reluctantly. "Well, sometimes he'd talk about hanging around the north side of the city, like he knew stuff that went on there."

"What stuff?"

"Like places to go, people to talk to. Then he'd get real secretive. He never said exactly who or where. I ignored him. I figured it was all bull."

"Nothing specific about the north side?"

"Nothing," he reiterated. But I got the impression he was holding back. I tried another angle.

"Where would he get money for running away?" I asked.

"Cash? None of us ever had much."

"His mom said he had a lot lately."

"I wouldn't know. Like I said, we weren't buddies anymore."

"Was he dealing drugs?"

"I don't know. Can I get back to work?"

"In a minute. Don't you want to help find him?"

"Well, sure, but I'm telling you all I know."

"What else would someone your age do to make money?" I mused aloud.

"Get a job," Greg said.

"Did Phil have a job? His mom didn't say so."

"Him! A regular job! He hated work. It's one of the things he fought about with his dad. But I tell you his dad hated it worse when—" he stopped abruptly.

"When what?" I asked. "If not a regular job then what kind did he have?"

Greg became even more nervous. "How do I get into this stuff?" I waited. Greg sighed disgustedly. "Okay. I don't know any of this for sure. That's the part that drove his dad nuts. When he started bringing home money, his dad would demand to know where it came from. Phil wouldn't tell him."

"And he told you?"

"Not really, but I think he used to do it with guys." Greg's face turned red. "According to Phil, the friends he used to brag about 'gave' him cash. I never really believed him.

Then when Lee said that stuff yesterday about Phil and the guy, I figured maybe he wasn't lying."

"Did he talk about these friends?"

"Nah, that's when he'd get all secretive. I figured he was probably dealing drugs. But I wasn't lying before. I really don't know for sure. Selling sex to adults is one way a kid can get lots of money. Some other kids do it too." Greg shook his head. "I shouldn't be telling you this stuff."

"Why not?"

"You're an adult. This can only lead to trouble."

"I'm trying to find the boy." I tried to think of what else to ask.

I was about to give up when Greg asked, "Mr. Mason, do people think Phil murdered his dad?"

"I don't know. The police talked to him once. When they find out he's gone, if they haven't already, they'll be suspicious. You realize he left only after his dad was murdered."

"This is some kind of hassle."

"Even without the death I would be concerned about the disappearance."

"He's almost eighteen. What's the big deal?"

"The deal is, Greg, that people care about him. His mom is worried." I tried a few other questions, but I'd gotten all I could out of him.

Half an hour later the kids were gone. Sylvester walked into my room. His hand shook as he raised it to adjust his glasses. Every time I saw him he looked more pasty white and nervous.

He started out all bluster. "I've had complaints about you bullying staff members. I won't have that, Mason. Plus we told you not to involve yourself in the Evans situation. We gave you a direct order about that."

I walked over to where he stood near the door. "You're my boss here, Sylvester, and anything connected to teaching and working conditions I will listen to, but neither you nor Armstrong have any say about my private conversations or activities. You never had. You never will."

His body sagged. Although the building was cool, sweat appeared on his upper lip. He moved to a student's desk and plopped his body into it. He wiped the sweat from his face with his handkerchief. When he spoke his voice was a pathetic whine. "Can't you for once see this from my point of view?"

"And what is that?" I asked in a neutral tone.

"I'm not an evil human being, although I'm sure you think so. I'm getting pressure from everyone constantly asking for answers I don't have. Why did this have to happen while I'm principal? I should never have quit teaching. I was happy in the classroom." He stood up abruptly, waved his arms dramatically. He said, "Do what you want. I don't care. It doesn't make any difference." He tottered to the door. Before he went out he turned back and said, "You'll be sorry, Mason."

I didn't bother puzzling about this threat.

Scott picked me up fifteen minutes later. He dropped me off at my place and went out to pick up dinner. We rarely cook for each other. Neither of us is good at it, although on special occasions he makes fabulous meals—Thanksgiving being one of his best. He's not bad at breakfasts either.

The doorbell rang while I set the table.

The cop, John Robertson, was at the door. I hesitated about letting him in. Scott would return any minute. I wasn't sure how Scott would react to the cop's presence. Depending on Robertson's intelligence and discretion, it could lead to Scott's being involved.

We sat in the living room. He began friendly enough, but all the same there was a note of menace underneath. "I checked into your background, Mr. Mason. You're an ex-marine. Did a tour of duty in Vietnam."

It's not something I talk about. I killed some human beings who were trying to kill me. A lot of screwed-up politicians tried to convince us this was a sane thing to do. Was it right or wrong? I prefer never to look back. I survived.

Robertson continued. "I like that about a guy. We've got to be tough in this day and age. We can't let these fucking intellectuals and faggots run things."

Big mistake on his part. I was furious, but held it in check for the moment until I knew what he wanted.

"What is it I can do for you, Detective?"

"I wanted to mention a few things. I have a couple questions." His demeanor remained placid, but I detected an increase in the harshness underneath. I might be a good guy because I was an ex-marine but as he shortly revealed, I was also a member of the pain-in-the-ass public getting in the way of his job.

He said, "I hear you've been taking quite an interest in this case."

"I don't see that as surprising."

"No, Mr. Mason, but it's usually the police who take care of asking questions and interviewing suspects. It's our job. We prefer not to be interfered with." The harshness in his voice increased. "Look, Mason, I'm telling you to back off. You're a veteran and all, but I want you to butt out. If you dare defy me—"

The front door opened. Scott walked in carrying dinner. He looked at the two of us. Scott solved the problem of recognition simply and without hesitation. He introduced himself. By shifting the packages, he could shake hands.

"Never thought I'd meet Scott Carpenter." Robertson sat back down slowly.

"Let me put these away and then I'll join you, if it's all right?" Scott asked.

"No problem," Robertson said. He gave me a surprised and confused look and gazed at me carefully. What he wanted to ask, I guessed, was why one of the biggest stars in baseball was in my living room.

Scott returned from the kitchen. "Can I get you something to drink, Detective, a beer maybe?"

"No, that's okay. I'm on duty, maybe another time."

"Sure thing." Scott gave him his dazzling smile and sat down next to me on the couch.

Robertson blurted out, "I'll never forget that second no-hitter in the World Series. It was fantastic. I watched every pitch on TV. I wish I could have been there."

"If we go to the Series again maybe I can get you tickets," Scott said. "I came in on the middle of something. How can we help you?"

"I came because Mr. Mason seems to have been conducting his own investigation of the Evans murder." His voice was more hurt than threatening, now that he was talking to a sports star. "We can't have interference, Mr. Carpenter."

"Call me Scott."

The cop swelled with pride of nearness to a hero. I figured him for a stroke in two minutes. I could already hear him telling the boys at the station house about his friend Scott Carpenter.

I hadn't liked his nasty tone when he started. I hated his fawning tone now. But I figured with him in this mood maybe I could get some information from him.

Scott said, "You see how it is. Tom's naturally concerned about what happened, knowing the family and the body being in his room."

"Of course," Robertson agreed.

I tried a question. "I was wondering, I never did hear, what exactly was it that killed him?"

The cop gave me a brief suspicious look.

Scott said, "When Tom described it to me I couldn't believe it. I kept trying to figure it out myself. I'd kind of like to know too, if you can tell us, that is. I know police seldom give out such information, but if you could see your way clear?" Scott's southern drawl was seldom more humble or persuasive.

The cop smiled. What I saw in that smile was—I'll do anything to please my hero. I might as well not have been there.

Robertson said, "I guess it wouldn't hurt to tell you a little. Although, really what I'm telling you gets sent to the press later today."

"We'd appreciate anything," Scott said.

Robertson began, "He'd been dead several hours when you found him. He was killed with a heavy blunt instrument. Whoever did it crushed his skull with repeated blows, but the medical people think the first blow probably was the one that did it. The killer kept hitting Evans long after he was dead."

"Do they know where he was killed?" I asked.

His expansive mood continued. "No. We haven't been able to trace his movements that night. He left home at nine P.M. He never came back. We haven't found his car or figured out what the hell he was doing in your classroom, or how he got there." He scratched his head. "He also had three thousand dollars on him when we examined him."

"Who do the police think did it?" I asked. The instant after I said it I knew I'd goofed.

He answered stiffly, "We're checking leads. We don't have anything firm yet."

"I'm sure you'll get something," Scott soothed quickly.

"We'll catch whoever did it, that's sure." He added, "Mr. Mason, you have to promise not to do any more interfering."

Scott spoke up. "I'm sure there won't be any problems."

I gave an ambiguous nod.

Robertson stood up. "I don't want to delay your dinner any longer." He spoke to me. "I'm glad I got this chance to talk to you." Then to Scott. "And got a chance to meet you."

Scott got up and shook the cop's hand. "And it's been a pleasure for me too." He walked the cop to the door.

Scott came back into the room. "I promised to get his kids an autographed baseball."

I said, "That son-of-a-bitching asshole."

"Don't let yourself get all worked up about him. He's an ordinary guy with a job to do."

"How can you defend him? He practically drooled all over you."

"You do that sometimes." He gave me a weak grin and sprawled his lanky frame next to me on the couch.

"At least I didn't start drooling the instant I met you, like he did. That fawning bullshit drives me nuts."

"You've seen it before."

"Yeah, and it usually doesn't bother me, but you weren't here for the first part of the conversation." I told him what Robertson said.

"He's an asshole," Scott agreed when I stopped.

He put his arm around me and drew me close.

"He'd be less impressed if he saw us now," I said.

"Should I ask him back? We could have him, his wife, and his kids over for a party. We could all be best friends."

I ignored his comment and said, "You handled him well."

He passed it off. "I've been handling fans and reporters for years."

"I meant the introduction, being here with me."

Scott shrugged. "What was to see? We didn't neck in front of him. Let him think what he wants."

I looked at him carefully. "You've changed. A couple years ago you'd have gone into a panic with what you walked in on."

Scott said, "This is your home. I shouldn't have to be scared of being gay here."

Scott and I met eight years ago. I remember it clearly. It was four-thirty on a gloomy November afternoon. It had alternately rained and sleeted since 8:00 A.M. I was in Unabridged Bookstore up on Broadway in Chicago in the gay section of town. It's my favorite bookstore in Chicago. I had two plastic bags crammed full of purchases. Halfway out the door I turned around to say good-bye to the owner. Not watching where I was going, I stumbled out the door and smacked into someone sheltering in the doorway. We both pitched over onto the pavement, the stranger on the bottom. I cursed. I tried getting up and fumbling for my scattered books at the same time. Rain poured down. Three of the books lay face open to the downpour. Then I noticed the blood on my victim's face. It seeped into his eyes faster than the rain could wash it away. He sat on the sidewalk looking dazed, not trying to get up. He must have hit his head hard, especially with me on top of him.

"You're bleeding" were my first words to him.

He touched his hand to his forehead, brought it to his eyes to look at the bloody mess. "Shit" was his first word to me.

The owner let us use the washroom in the store to clean up. When we finished cleaning, I apologized again. I buttoned my coat, put on my gloves, and picked up my packages. I turned to go.

At this point he said very softly, "Wait, please."

I noticed how deep the voice was, along with the southern drawl. I remember turning around and gazing into his deep blue eyes for an eternity. Eventually his face turned red in embarrassment.

"Are you gay?" he blurted out.

"Are you taking a survey?" I answered.

He looked bewildered. "I'm asking because—" He

stopped. "I only—" He stopped again. He hung his head like a first grader in trouble with a favorite teacher. "Forget it," he mumbled.

I guessed he was a severe closet case, and I didn't know if I wanted to be involved in his coming out. But he was good-looking, and it was cold and raining, and I was responsible for his injury. He looked like a bedraggled puppy. I felt sorry for him.

"Let me buy you a cup of coffee," I said.

"Nah, it's okay," he said.

But I insisted and reluctantly he agreed. We walked the half block to the Melrose Restaurant. It wasn't odd when he asked to sit far in the back away from the windows.

From that first cup of coffee, once he relaxed, he was a lot of fun to be with. I've never felt more relaxed and at ease than when I'm with him, and it started that day. Besides, he makes me laugh. He's the funniest man on earth.

People have asked if I recognized him right away. I didn't. Even when he told me his last name I didn't associate it with a baseball player. He was known, of course, but he wasn't anywhere near as famous then as he is now. In fact, it was three months before he told me what he really did for a living. At first he said he was a part-time manager of an exercise club, which was true. The imminent arrival of spring training and his need for leaving precipitated the revelation of his actual occupation. I told him I wasn't prejudiced and didn't care what his job preference was. Even after three months, I think he feared I'd call all the media and announce our relationship.

For the first few years, even before fame and its attendant difficulties, Scott was paranoid about us being seen in public together. I pointed out to him that lots of guys who aren't gay go to movies, have meals together. He'd gotten better over the years, but I think he still worried when we went out around my place. Usually we went out in Chicago. There were more and better places to go, and I think he felt more comfortable there. For some reason he was less likely to be recognized for who he was in the city than around River's Edge.

"What I want you to explain to me," Scott said, "is why you didn't tell him about Sylvester or any of the rest of what you know?"

"He pissed me off."

"Yeah, me too, but he's the cop. They're supposed to handle this stuff."

"I know but"—I sat up from his embrace—"he made me so damn mad. Besides, I don't really know anything. I've got some information maybe, but really, it's mostly rumor. I've got no hard evidence."

"The stuff you know could help them," Scott insisted. "You've got to tell them."

"All right, I'll call Frank Murphy tomorrow and tell him."

He eyed me warily. "You're planning on doing more than looking for Phil?" It wasn't so much a question as a statement.

He knows me well. "Yeah, I guess I am," I admitted.

"I was afraid of that. Look, Tom, there's only trouble in this for you. You might get hurt. The police don't want interference. Somebody took a shot at you. Your boss is pissed."

"My boss is petrified out of his mind, but I can't figure out why yet."

"Maybe he killed him."

"An administrator? Be serious. One of them wouldn't have the courage to kill anybody."

"It was a suggestion," Scott replied with some asperity.

"Sorry," I said.

He took my hand and continued. "Tom, I really am worried. I wish you wouldn't start."

"I've already started. I'm going to find Phil and the murderer."

His shoulders slumped in discouragement. "There's no way I can talk you out of it?"

"No."

"Okay," he said, "but if you're going on, I'm going to stick with you. One of us has to be sensible in this."

"Thanks, I appreciate that, I think."

Over dinner we discussed the conversation with Robertson some more.

"You know," I said, "what I find curious is that he didn't mention about Phil being missing."

"Maybe he doesn't know."

"When they find out the kid's gone his rating as a suspect will soar."

"Yeah," Scott agreed. "What I wonder is where the car is?"

"That one I think is easy. I bet it's in some alley in Chicago soon to be covered with tons of snow, never to be heard of again."

When we finished cleaning up after dinner Scott asked, "What's next?"

"I'll make some phone calls to my gay friends. They should be able to give me some leads on runaway gay kids. Neil Spirakos has his fingers in every community pie. I haven't talked to him in a while. He paid his way through college by hustling. He ought to be able to help, or point us in the right direction if nothing else."

Neil was in when I called. He agreed to meet us at nine-thirty that night. At Scott's insistence, I tried to call Frank Murphy. He was off duty. I left a message.

We met at the Melrose. Neil announced in a loud voice, "I want to sit right down in front so I can watch all the gorgeous boys walk by."

The corner booth, where you could gaze through the

broad front windows, was empty. We settled in. Scott and I on one side, Neil on the other.

"I want you both to know how unchic it is these days to be seen in the Melrose before two A.M. The reigning queens meet here at two-thirty each morning. You can't imagine what a favor I'm doing you boys. I don't know what this will do to my reputation."

Years before I'd worked with Neil on several gay activist committees. Gone were the pretty-boy looks of youth that paid his way through college and ultimately into the business world. At forty-three his hairline had receded as rapidly as his paunch expanded. His looks came more often now from a bottle. Years ago a grateful client left him a bankrupt company in his will—a waste disposal operation. Neil took it and made it a million-dollar business. He knew the dirt on half the prominent closeted gays in the city, and all the dirt on the uncloseted ones.

"We need information, Neil," I said.

"I have that in abundance, but first tell me, dears, where have you been keeping yourselves?" He patted Scott's hand. "Have you been keeping this gorgeous hunk"—he flipped a wrist at me—"chained in some suburban mall? If the rest of us can't have him, you should at least share him."

Scott withdrew his hand and said nothing.

Neil turned to me. "And how is teaching? Do the little no-neck monsters still occupy your precious time?"

"Still."

He gave a dramatic sigh. "So what is it you dears want? You were terribly mysterious on the phone, Thomas."

I hate it when somebody calls me Thomas. It reminds me of my mother, and she only used it when I'd done something wrong.

"It's not like you to play cat and mouse. Of course, I know this isn't a simple social call. That would be too much to expect. You haven't called in ages."

"Your phone doesn't have a dial?" I asked. He hadn't called either.

Over the years we'd drifted apart, his charm getting less as his riches increased. His rarely veiled antagonism to Scott made it worse. Yet under it all, he was a good person. Plus he had information I wanted.

I told him about the murder and what I'd learned since. He listened shrewdly and attentively.

I ended, "What I need to know is where to start. If Phil's hustling, where to look. If he's working for an escort service, who to talk to. If possible, find out where he's staying."

"You don't want much do you?"

"I need to find the kid," I said flatly.

He gave his dramatic sigh. "Okay. You're not sure he's hustling?"

"Right."

"Or even if he's gay?"

"Pretty positive about that."

"Or if he's in this city or several thousand miles away?"

"Yeah."

He shook his head. "I don't think you realize the size of the task ahead of you. We're not even talking needle-in-a-haystack here. We haven't even found the haystack. Why would the kid stay in cold Chicago if he could hustle in warm L.A.?"

"He promised his brother he'd come get him, and I'm not convinced he had the money to leave."

"Sugar daddies provide all kinds of benefits. If he's as good-looking as you say he could hitchhike easily. He could be anywhere."

"I've got to start somewhere."

"I remember you always were big on hopeless cases."

"That's why we're still friends, isn't it?" I smiled.

"You're lucky I still can't resist that sexy smile, but don't press your luck," he replied.

I returned to the issue at hand. "Do you know where he'd stay?"

"Anywhere. He could be with some sugar daddy and never be seen on the streets."

"Is there somebody in the gay community who specializes in helping runaways?"

"Not anymore. There used to be a few ad hoc volunteer groups, but they've gone by the wayside. Most gay men shy away from involvement with young people. They're afraid the cops would think they were in it only to get into the pants of jail bait."

"How about if he's working for a service?"

"That's a little more delicate. There are only a couple that deal in kids, and they tend to be very far underground."

Scott broke in, "Those pimps should be arrested and hanged. They're ruining kids' lives."

"And we're applying for sainthood?" Neil pointed his finger at Scott. "For many your very existence as a gay man makes you the equal of child molesters and kiddie peddlers. I can picture the self-righteous columnists—how can this man play baseball and be an example for kids when he sucks cock?" Neil looked disgusted. "Morality has little to do with it. Sick child molesters have been with us since we climbed out of the slime. They'll continue to be so. At any rate, moralizing isn't going to find the kid."

"I only meant—" Scott began.

Neil patted his hand again. "Be still, dear, you're awful cute, but we have work to do." He turned to me.

I saw Scott getting red with anger. He held it in. Neil made some demeaning crack every time he saw Scott. I began to protest. Neil stopped me. "Do you want information or not?"

Scott gave my leg a reassuring squeeze under the table to let me know it was all right to let it drop.

I swallowed my anger and nodded at Neil. "The escort services," I reminded him.

"Ah, yes, well, there're two that might employ him. I can discreetly check that for you. I'll probably get honest answers from them, although I can't guarantee it."

"Do you know anyplace a youngster might stay or hang out? I know the young hustler bar used to be the Dump on Lower Wacker Drive."

"Not anymore. The place to find a young hustler is the Womb."

I hadn't heard of the place. "Where's that?" I asked.

"It's on Clark Street south of Diversy, across from the post office."

I'd been past the corner but never noticed the bar. "I think we'll head down there and ask around," I said.

He gave me a pitying look. "Do you think anyone in such a bar would answer questions? After you ask the first one the bar will probably clear out. They'll assume you're cops. And if you're thinking of waiting for Phil to show up, forget it. Your chances of being there simultaneously are minimal."

"We have to start somewhere," I said.

"Good luck," he said doubtfully.

"How soon can you check those services?" I asked.

"I'll call you tomorrow, Sunday at the latest."

I said a brief thanks and we left. It was nearly eleven-thirty. It was less than a mile to the bar. We decided to walk. I could tell Scott was angry. After a few blocks I said, "There was no call for him to talk to you that way."

He shrugged his shoulders and said, "It's not important."

The Womb was in the basement of a crumbling building. The color scheme could most kindly be described as hideous. The lighting, what little there was, revolved and twirled slowly. It managed to pick up the most lurid tints, generally suggesting walls spray-painted with vomit. The entertainment consisted of a gargantuan woman, three-hundred pounds at least, leather clad from toe to crown, slowly doing a striptease on top of the bar. While we were there, in a unique twist, after taking it all off, she put it back on, then off, then on. Perhaps it was an eternal statement. She moved, you couldn't call it dancing, and stripped, out of time to the music, which in itself redefined the word loud.

People jammed the room. In dim corners men kissed and groped each other. I only looked long enough to ascertain if Phil was so engaged. As far as I could see he wasn't. As we squeezed to the bar, two stools emptied in front of us. We grabbed them.

Across from where we sat was the exception to the lighting. There, in an area hidden from the door, light bathed a wall in blinding whiteness for the space of about fifteen feet. In this space were men. Most were young, all were good-looking, some were beautiful. They were tight jeaned, leather clad, preppie, or any style a customer might want. They stared vacantly ahead. Sporadically one of the posing men strolled casually into the dimness. Men exchanged desires, struck deals, and left. On the wall next to the exit door was a condom machine vending several well-known brands.

None of the men in the light was Phil Evans.

The bartender was flat stomached, heavily muscled, and ruggedly handsome. I guessed him to be around twenty-five. He wore no shirt. A gold earring topped with a tiny diamond pierced his left nipple. A silver ring with a cluster of feathers clinging to it pierced the right one. His jeans clung tighter than cellophane and clearly showed the placement of his dick and balls. He smiled at us. "What'll you guys have?" I barely heard his shout.

I ordered a diet soda and Scott a light beer.

The bartender returned with our drinks. "Anything else I can get for you?" His smile was now a leer. I felt Scott move closer to me, his knee pressing tightly against mine.

I shook my head no to the bartender. He winked and left. Resting his lips on my ear, Scott yelled as gently as possible, "What the hell do we do?" Even that close it was hard to hear him.

I pulled his head over to yell back. We carried on the conversation in this odd manner, mouth to ear, throughout. "We wait," I yelled, then asked, "are you nervous about being in here?"

He smiled faintly and shook his head. He said, "I don't believe I'm in such a place. No one else would believe I was either." We were both aware that if there was a police raid both of our careers could be in trouble. If they decided to raid a gay bar, this would be the one.

For a painful three hours we stuck it out. Phil never came in. By three o'clock the place cleared out a little. The bartender was unbusy for the first time that night. I decided to try a few questions. I motioned him over. "We're looking for someone," I said.

"Isn't everybody?" he responded.

"A specific kid."

He eyed me carefully then smiled. "It takes all types. I wouldn't think it of you. Forget kids. What you want is a man." He flexed his muscles, dropped his voice, and moved closer. He spoke so only I could hear. "Why don't you ditch your friend here and stick around? I get off soon. You don't need to buy one of these creeps. Hell, you could be on the wall and make a fortune yourself. And you can have me for free."

"Thanks, but no thanks," I said. "We're looking for a specific kid, a runaway. His name is Phil Evans. Do you know him?" I regretted not bringing a picture.

The bartender drew away immediately. He gave us a suspicious look. "What is this? Are you guys cops?"

I assured him we weren't but his eyes remained doubtful. He was called away to fix some drinks and didn't return.

It was Friday night and the bar would be open to four A.M. I didn't see any point in hanging around until closing. I also didn't see any use in randomly picking customers to question without a picture. Tomorrow I'd try talking to some of the people against the wall.

We spent the night in Scott's Lake Shore Drive penthouse. Saturday we awoke at eleven. I hadn't brought any clothes so I put on a pair of Scott's jockey shorts, socks, jeans, and one of his old University of Arizona sweatshirts.

Over coffee Scott asked, "What's on the schedule today?"

"I want to stop by my place and get a picture of Phil. I want to talk with the former social worker. We've had a new one every year for the last three. I've got an old faculty phone list somewhere at home. I'll call Frank Murphy as soon as we're done with breakfast. Plus I hope Neil calls so we can check on the escort services today. Then tonight I think we should try to get to the bar earlier."

"How early?"

"Maybe around nine. I doubt if it gets busy much before that."

He glanced at his calendar on the refrigerator. "I've got a speaking engagement tonight. It's a kids' hospital benefit. I don't want to miss it."

"That's okay. I can go early by myself and wait for you there."

"I'd rather we go together later."

I thought his worries about me were groundless. "Scott, there's been no further attack since Wednesday. After a while it's going to get impossible for us to always be together."

"For now though I think there's still danger."

"All right." I gave in.

He went into the utility room and came back with four shoe boxes, each overflowing with autographed baseballs.

"Why don't we stop by the police station instead of calling. I could deliver these to Robertson in person."

I pointed at the stuffed boxes. "I remember you saying he asked for one. We aren't thinking of bribery here?"

"Well"—he grinned at me—"we'll call it a gift."

"I didn't know you kept a supply of those around."

"I bring a few with me to speaking engagements. You get all kinds of requests to autograph stuff—menus, napkins, autograph books, people's casts, stuff like that. You can't give a baseball to each of them, but a lot of times there's a special program or a special kid they're honoring. Like the Little League batting champ, or a kid who's sick, or somebody gets a father of the year award, like that. I like to give them something special. They get a big kick out of it. It costs me a little extra, but you should see their faces light up."

I watched him rummaging through the boxes. "Don't use all those on the cops."

"I wasn't going to. A few should do it."

I ran my eyes over his body as he crossed the kitchen to return the boxes to the storage room. He reappeared in the doorway, came back to the table, saw me watching him.

He smiled. "And what are you looking at?"

"The way your pants cling to the curves of your ass then around the front to the tight folds around your zipper that outline your—"

He leaned down, kissed me, gave a sex growl, lifted me from the chair.

*　　　*　　　*

First we stopped at the police station. It was a two-story faded yellow brick building. The dirt on the windows didn't look as if it had been cleaned since they put it up forty years ago.

Inside it was like old home week. Every cop in the place shook Scott's hand.

Frank Murphy drew me aside. In his office he gave me a wry look. "You're fortunate your buddy Carpenter has impressed everyone, especially Robertson."

"Everyone except you?"

"I'm impressed, sort of. I think you can be of valuable help in this. I've worked with you. The problem we might have with you is you care too much. That might lead you to do something foolish. If you find something out, Tom, I need to hear it."

I nodded. "I'll be careful. About learning anything—" I paused.

He said, "Did you know somebody broke into the Evans house Wednesday, probably around noon?"

"No. Do you think it's connected to the break-in at my classroom?"

"Maybe." He looked thoughtful, then said, "Phil wasn't at the funeral this morning." He gave me a keen glance. "He seems to be missing."

I was about to tell him everything when the door burst open with a crash.

Scott entered with an arm draped around Robertson's shoulder. The cop held two autographed baseballs in his hand. "Look at these, Frank, this guy's great, like a regular guy."

Frank smiled indulgently.

Robertson continued. "I'm glad these guys stopped by. Did I tell you, Frank, they agreed to stop playing amateur detective and leave things to the police?"

"You did mention something about that this morning."

"Oh, yeah, so I did."

Frank gave me a hard stare. "It's a warning I'm sure they took to heart, and if they did stumble onto something, they'd call us first thing."

"Sure they would. Look at these baseballs—my boys will go nuts."

Robertson's reappearance brought back all my stubbornness. I decided to wait until I knew a little more, then tell them everything.

In the car I told Scott that the police knew about Phil. I mentioned the break-in at the Evanses'. He was as puzzled as I, and it added to his concern. I figured there had to be a connection, but I couldn't begin to understand what.

Scott interrupted my reverie. "You didn't tell him, did you?"

"There wasn't time, what with cops falling all over you." I rationalized, "For the moment our concern is the whereabouts of the kid, not the murder itself."

"The cops won't see it that way."

"No, I suppose not. We've got a full evening to cope with. Let's concentrate on that."

At home I cut a picture of Phil from an old yearbook. I tried calling Neil, but there was no answer. I called Heather Delacroix, the former social worker, and set up an appointment for the next afternoon. After we worked out, Scott went to his dinner. I read some of Boorstin's *The Discoverers*.

We arrived at the bar at ten-thirty. The three-hundred-pound woman in leather still danced. In addition to last night's costume she wore a spiked helmet, a leather hook, spike pasties, and two-inch-wide dog collars up and down her arms. The problem was she didn't look out of place. The Saturday night crowd here made the creatures in the bar scene in *Star Wars* look normal. Only in the Womb, they would serve androids too.

I tried asking a few customers questions. Most of them hurriedly moved away before I finished asking or explaining. A few at least looked at the picture. They shrugged, looked down, to the side, anywhere but at me. They mumbled their negatives and shuffled awkwardly away.

At eleven-fifteen the stripper lumbered off. I assumed it was time for the bar to get a break from holding up all that weight. She came over to where we leaned against a dark wall. Up close the planes and folds of her skin glowed with sweat. She didn't chew gum, but should have. She held her hood in her hand. Sequins glittered in her black hair. She looked to be about thirty. She gave a smile that radiated unfriendliness.

"Can I help you boys?" she asked. Her voice was remarkably clear and crisp, cutting through the music without shouting.

"We're looking for someone, a kid, maybe you know him."

She broke in, "I don't like people bothering my customers. I've gotten complaints. Some of them think you're cops."

"We really need to find him. His family is worried."

"So? All the families in the world are worried about their lost lambs. Maybe if they worried sooner they wouldn't be lost. Me, I'm worried because you're bad for business."

Frustrated but undaunted, I tried to show her Phil's picture. She wouldn't look at it.

"I want you guys to leave, now, before I have to get rough. If you're cops produce some I.D. and charge me. Either way let's move it." Her biceps expanded and contracted, squeezing the tightened leather. She clamped her hand on my arm preparatory to ushering me toward the exit. I tried to break her grip, but couldn't. Scott placed his hand on her wrist and held on. It was strength against bulk. Each strained against the other. A major blow up could scatter the already skittish clientele. Abruptly her grip on my arm loosened. She gave Scott a dirty look. "You some kind of professional?" she asked.

"Yeah," he said.

I rubbed my arm where she'd grabbed me. She rubbed hers where Scott had applied pressure. The bartender appeared. "Any trouble, Daphne?" he asked.

"Nothing I can't handle," she answered.

I looked around the bar. If anyone noticed our little scene they gave no indication.

"What's your interest in this?" she demanded. "You the father, uncle, mother's boyfriend, disappointed customer, jealous boyfriend?"

"I was the boy's teacher."

"You're the teacher? And you're going to this trouble?" For the first time she began to look less belligerent. She eyed me thoughtfully. "Follow me." She jerked her head toward the rear of the bar.

We climbed down two flights of dimly lit wooden stairs. At the bottom we turned left, through a door marked DANGER HIGH VOLTAGE. But the only sign of electricity inside was a single bare bulb painted red, attached in a socket above the door. Three chairs sat in the middle of the clothes-strewn room. From one of the heaps of clothes she took a red silk cape and flung it over her bulk. She billowed like a tent in a high wind when she twirled to overburden a chair. With a lighter that matched the color of her cape she lit an un-filtered Camel cigarette.

She peered up at us. "Who are you two?" she demanded.

I introduced us. She gave no sign of recognition at Scott's name. She motioned us to the other chairs. We three sat in the glimmer of the red light. I explained, "We need to find a kid, an eighteen-year-old, named Phil Evans. He's run away. He's probably a suspect in a murder." I gave her the picture.

She looked at it and handed it back to me.

"Why don't you let the family handle it, or the cops?"

"The family's a mess. His dad is the one who was mur-dered. His mom asked us for help. The cops are more wor-ried about the murder. We care about the kid."

"A teacher busting his butt for his kids. Corny, but I like it." She waved her cigarette at me. "I used to be a teacher. I taught for five years." She laughed. "I made more money my first year as owner of this bar than in all five of those years put together."

"You own this place?" Scott asked.

"Do you think I'd be allowed to do that tawdry little act if I didn't?"

"You've got a point there," Scott said.

She ignored his comment and continued. "But I didn't quit teaching because of the money. I taught high school." She dragged deeply on her cigarette. "I loved kids. I think I really helped them. They used to come back and thank me for the help I'd given them. So why'd I quit? The cash was adequate. It was one of those rumor things. Someone—kids, teachers, parents—who knows—and it doesn't make much difference where it started—began to spread rumors about me. Eventually everybody knew I was a lesbian.

"Then it got ugly. I got in a major fight with my department head. She hated it that kids liked me better. She threatened to tell the principal, superintendent, and school board that I was a lesbian if I wouldn't knuckle under. I laughed at her and dared her to do her worst. Then she threatened to say I seduced little girls. She laughed at me. She said she didn't need proof. A simple accusation like that would ruin my career.

"I'll never forget the astonished look on her wrinkled old face when I belted her one. The punch broke her jaw. She sued. I agreed to quit if she dropped the case. She did, so I left."

She lit another cigarette from the butt of the last one. "So what difference does that little story make? I guess it means I understand a teacher who cares, because I thought of myself as one. I'm going to help you."

"Great," I said.

"Don't get too excited. I'll help in that I'll tell Phil you've been looking for him. If he wants to see you, I'll set up an appointment. If not, forget it."

"But you do know where he is?" Scott asked.

She gave him a sour grimace. "Of course, or how could I tell him?"

"You're not worried about the police?" I asked.

"You're here. They're not. I assume that means you know something they don't. I assume in exchange for my little help you keep your mouths shut."

We agreed.

"Good, now I want you to leave my customers alone. Come back tomorrow afternoon around five. I'll have definite information."

We got up to leave. "Thank you, Daphne," I said.

She stubbed out the last of her chain-smoked cigarettes. "Daphne's my stage name. My real name is Janet Stewart."

Outside the bar Scott put a hand on my arm and stopped me. "We've got to do something. She knows where the kid is."

I scrunched deeper into my jacket against the biting wind that blew off Lake Michigan.

"What could we do?" I asked him.

"Call the cops."

"We gave our word. Besides, she'd deny everything."

"There were two of us. I'm a witness. She can't deny saying it."

"I think she could, and get away with it. She's smart. She knows we want the kid. And she knows the cops around here. You can bet on that. We're amateurs. She's a pro. I doubt if we'd stand a chance."

We stopped at Fullerton and Clark to wait for a walk signal.

Scott asked abruptly, "What if she's lying?"

"I don't picture that. She didn't have to admit anything to us, and she did. No, I don't see why she would." I shivered. "I think we should trust her for now. She trusted us. I'll give her the benefit of the doubt."

"What if she really does know and something happens to the kid? We're partly responsible."

"I'm open to suggestions, preferably in the warmth of your penthouse." It was too damn cold to be arguing in the middle of the sidewalk. "There's nothing we can do until tomorrow."

* * *

Sunday morning at eleven-thirty Neil called.

"I've got some information for you," he said.

"We found out some things too."

"Me first, dear. I'm enjoying being detective. I must apologize for taking so long to get back to you, but mother was prying into many deep dark little closets. One can't be too careful in these matters. First the escort services. None of the reputable ones have heard a thing about the kid."

"Could they be holding out on you?"

"Possible but not probable. Beyond these services there are several prominent call-boy groups, assorted pimps, and independents. I think the actual house of prostitution is somewhat anachronistic in this day and age. None of the above ever heard of the kid either. That doesn't mean there isn't some lesser-known or newer group he's working for, or like I said the other night, the kid could be freelancing."

"So you didn't get anything."

"Be not too hasty, gorgeous one. I went back and checked several of the disreputable escort services. That was much more difficult. One of them had this tidbit. They never heard of a Phil Evans, but they knew Jim Evans. I was sure it wasn't the same man. Who ever heard of a forty-six-year-old hustler? I described the elder Evans from what you told me. My source insisted that it was the same man. He didn't know what Evans did for the service. He only knew there was some connection."

"What would Jim Evans have to do with a gay escort service?" I asked.

"That I couldn't tell you."

"Could you at least tell me which escort service it was?"

He mulled this over. "I suppose it wouldn't hurt. I know you can't reveal my source, and you won't reveal where you got this from."

I assured him I wouldn't.

He warned, "It's unrealistic to expect to call and expect them to talk to you."

"I've got to try."

"When we worked together, you were the most trustworthy one, often the only trustworthy one. Use this information carefully. It's called Adonis-at-Large. It specializes in pretty young men. Be careful when you call them," he said. "It's most likely they'll simply hang up on you, but there's a real possibility of danger when you start getting nosy around those prostitution things."

"You're involved with them," I pointed out.

"Yes, dear, but that's different. I'm involved in the community and have well-connected sources whom I trust and who trust me."

"Would you be willing to come with me if I decided to go see them?"

"No. I can't go beyond my sources, sorry."

"Thanks anyway. I'll be careful."

"Good. Now, I've also checked at every point available to me in the general community: social service agencies, hotlines, whatever. As far as they know or were willing to tell, the kid isn't in Chicago. Sorry, dear, that's not what you wanted to hear, I know. Tell me, what did you learn?"

"We might have a lead from a three-hundred-pound lesbian named Daphne."

"Janet, from the Womb?"

"You know her?"

"I know a great deal about her." His voice dripped the acid

of a vicious queen on the attack. "Don't trust that woman. Better yet, have no dealings with that woman."

"Why not?"

"She has the most foul reputation of any so-called community leader in the city. She's double-crossed half the prominent gays in town and all the bar owners."

"Double-crossed?"

"The examples are legion. Here's the major problem. Say they'd all get together to endorse a candidate for office, or to deal with police raids on our bars. They'd agree on united action. A few days later, sometimes only hours later, they'd find out that she'd cut her own deal with the alderman, the ward committeeman, or the commander down at the local police station. To say she's intensely disliked is an understatement. Don't expect much help from her. She's got one of the most prosperous bars in the community, and she never spends a cent on any gay causes."

"She might be able to lead us to the kid."

"She told you that?"

"She said she'd talk to him and let us know if he would talk to us."

"Don't believe her. Anyway I haven't gotten to the worst. She's one of the disreputable crowd I couldn't check on. My sources wouldn't even talk about her. I do know this. She's got boys working out of that bar, and we're talking *young* boys. What's more, she's never been raided, not even harassed slightly. She's got to have powerful connections."

"Does she actually own the bar?" I asked. "She said she did."

"I doubt it. She runs the place and may own a part of it. It's more likely a partnership deal. Most of them are these days."

After a dozen more warnings and predictions of doom, Neil rang off, insisting we keep in touch with him.

Scott had listened on an extension. He came into the living room. "What do we do now?"

"About Daphne?" I shrugged. "I don't know. She seemed okay last night."

"Do you trust Neil?"

"Yes, and I've known him for years, but we don't have much else for a lead. We'll have to be careful, that's all."

He agreed glumly.

We talked over what I should say when I called the escort service. We couldn't decide on specific action. I dialed the number Neil gave me and asked for Jim Evans. The person on the other end said I must have the wrong number. There was no one there by that name. I hung up, looked at Scott. "Nothing," I told him.

I checked my watch. "If we're meeting Heather Delacroix in an hour out in Orland we better get moving."

We dressed and drove to Heather's. She'd worked in the district the year before. I'd heard she quit to work for a private agency at a much higher salary. When I talked to her the day before, she had reluctantly agreed to my request for a meeting.

She lived in the last condominium in one of the new subdivisions just south of Orland Park, a block east of 94th Avenue. She took our coats and offered us coffee and tea. We sat in the living room on a brown vinyl couch. Stuffed elephants of varying sizes, shapes, and colors decorated a few small tables and shelves. Heather was in her mid-twenties, with red hair and a frown that denoted seriousness of purpose.

She began preemptorially, "I looked through my files on the Evans family, although I hardly needed to refresh my memory. I've made some decisions. If you can do something to help that poor family, then I want to be a part of it."

"Great," I said.

First she talked about Mr. Evans, most of which I already

knew from Meg, although Heather had more details. Then she talked about the Evans kids.

"The girls seem normal. Since we're in a kindergarten-through twelfth-grade district, I was able to observe them in class. From what I saw, and what the teachers said, there was no need to refer them for testing.

"The eighth grader, Keith, is another story. He's very interested in sports. The coach said he is an average player. Academically he has numerous learning problems. He's been in learning disability classes since second grade. The father opposed that placement. From what I could find out this was one of the few times Mom stood up to Dad. If this was what was best for the child—she wanted it."

"But he's still in the program after all these years?" I asked.

"Yes."

"Wait," Scott interrupted. "What's learning disabled? The kid seemed strange to me the other night."

"How so?" Heather asked.

Scott explained his unease over the boy's reaction to his dad's death.

When he finished she said, "I don't find anything extraordinary in his reaction. Each of us reacts differently to the death of a loved one. Some never cry at all. With the dynamics in that family one could expect almost anything. Being learning disabled would have no connection to his reaction to his father's death."

Scott nodded that he understood. Heather continued. "I talked with Keith a few times. He hasn't developed the belligerence of many L.D. kids. He seems quite benign about it. He works very hard in school. The L.D. teacher reported him as being very cooperative. They seriously considered dropping him from the program this year and, if not, then surely in high school."

I said, "I tried to find out about this year. The social worker threw me out of her office."

"Did she?" Heather gave a wry smile. "She's new. She's young. She's not used to the pressure, but I'll get to that." "Was Keith a victim of abuse?" I asked.

She sighed. "There was no physical evidence, no bruises. Yet I found it hard to believe that Evans attacked only the older boy."

"What did you find out about Phil?"

She pulled her sweater closer around her. "I couldn't get him to open up. I went to his father. I felt extremely uncomfortable going to him, but something had to be done. It was a disaster. He told me he didn't believe in this psychological bullshit. I phoned the mother. She was vague and distant. I couldn't get any answers out of her. Neither parent seemed willing to take an active part in what happened to their son." She shook her head sorrowfully. "Maybe if I'd had more experience I could have helped that family."

"I don't know if anyone could have helped them," I said.

"At any rate, next I went to see Sylvester. Phil's case disturbed me. I wanted further testing done, and more followups on the family in general."

"What did Sylvester do?" I asked.

Her eyes misted with tears. "I was a first-year social worker, right out of college, exceptionally well trained, I thought. I wanted to help that family. I didn't trust the father at all. I feared for the little girls. Sylvester did everything and nothing. He promised immediate action. He agreed with me fully. He cautioned me about a staff member being involved, but assured me action would be taken."

"What happened?"

"Nothing, and the harder I worked the more nothing happened. I did all the paperwork, turned it in. First Sylvester needed time to review it. He was busy, but would get to it soon. Then his secretary had it for typing. Next it was lost and I had to resubmit all the paperwork. Then he couldn't get parental signatures. There was more paperwork so that we could do follow-ups without parental permission. That work had to be sent through the bureaucracy—the superintendent, and the Special Education co-op. It went everywhere and got nowhere. I went to see him countless times."

She ran her hand through her hair. "I met a stone wall. I tried going to Armstrong. All I got from him was double talk. I was totally frustrated. It had to be all Sylvester's doing. I watched other cases go through his office in normal amounts of time. Sure, there are always some delays, but it's usually less than a month, two at the most.

"So brave me went in to confront Sylvester." She gave a short, bitter laugh. "You know what he told me? The bastard talked about my evaluation and the possibility of an unsatisfactory rating. He totally ignored what I had to say. I felt completely helpless and furiously angry at the same time. This was around mid-March. I decided to finish the year, but I handed in my resignation the next day. I don't have to work under those conditions."

"So the rumor that you quit for a better-paying job was untrue?"

"Yes. It was another of Sylvester's lies."

"Sylvester covered up for or protected Evans. I wonder why?"

"I never could figure it out. They didn't seem like close friends."

I told her what Leonard Vance said about meetings between Evans and the two administrators.

She walked over to the sliding glass doors and stared out. "That family was so sad." She turned back to us. "I really had nothing to go on. No neighbors complained. The boys had some trouble, but weren't out of control in any way. Dad was strange. Mom seemed to be a basket case. I had a horrible feeling about it." She sat back down slowly. "It turns out I was right."

We listened to a grandfather clock ticking in another room. A few moments later I broke the silence. "When I tried to talk to Nancy Lacey, she seemed frightened."

"She probably was. I've talked with her a few times. She's a nice kid, from a proper school, terribly sincere, wants to change the world. I know the type well. I was exactly like her. She's probably under even more pressure than I was. I presume Sylvester got to her very early to warn her away from the Evans family. She didn't strike me as the type who could buck that kind of pressure."

We stayed another half hour but learned nothing else new. While saying thank yous and good-byes we promised to keep her informed of any new developments.

The meeting with Daphne was for five. I didn't want to be late.

There were no customers in the Womb. Daphne was behind the bar. "Gentlemen, you are in luck." She pointed at me. "You must be one hell of a teacher. Not only did the kid agree to see you, he's eager. I had to restrain him from coming down here. Honorable as you may be, I thought I'd wait to see if you came in trailing a herd of police. Let's go."

She grabbed a black leather purse off the bar and pushed past us toward the exit. "I hope you guys have exact change," she called as she went out the door.

She marched us south on Clark Street. At Fullerton we caught a westbound bus. When the bus stopped under the el tracks, she grabbed us and pulled us out the door. She hurried up to the el platform, watching behind us suspiciously. After an hour of switching buses and trains, and finally taking a cab, we wound up on Wacker Drive at the base of the Sears Tower. On a Sunday at six, except for a stray tourist or two, it was deserted. We went to one of the fast-food restaurants across the street. A CLOSED sign hung in the window.

She ignored it and went right in. She flipped the lock on the door when we were inside.

Phil Evans sat in a booth at the back of the restaurant. We sat down across from him. Daphne stood. "I'm going to be sitting up front," she said. "No trouble or double crosses. The manager here and I are friends." She pointed to a man emerging from the shadows behind the counter. His expensive suit didn't hide the muscles bulging on his six-foot six-inch frame. "We can handle even your muscular boyfriend if we have to." I had no intention of starting anything. I was glad to find the kid.

Phil was a handsome boy, very much like his father. He wore a dark-brown corduroy suit that looked brand-new and expensive. Phil smiled at me. "Isn't Daphne something?"

I said, "Yes, she is. It's good to see you, Phil."

I introduced Scott. He recognized the name.

Phil's smile brightened. He said, "Is what Daphne told me this morning true? Are you gay, Mr. Mason? Are you guys lovers?"

Scott flinched. There was little point in lying. I told him yes.

"Wow, I'd never have guessed. You're so masculine and normal acting." He blushed. "I didn't mean anything by that, Mr. Mason."

"I know, Phil. I'll take it as a compliment." I said, "People have been worried about you. We've been looking all over for you."

"I'm glad it was you that came looking for me. I've always trusted you. Remember the time the pack of cigarettes fell out of my jacket, and you took them away but never turned me in to the office? That was cool. In class you always talked to us like we were people. We had to work hard and you were a pain in the butt sometimes, but hey, I learned a lot." While we talked his hands fluttered jerkily adjusting his collar, cuffs, and tie. Under the table his left leg jiggled in constant motion. The kid was tightly strung. He saw me noticing his clothes.

"Nice, huh?"

"Very nice. You seem to be doing well since you left home."

"You bet. I'm never going back." He sounded confident.

"Your mom is worried about you."

His temper flared. "I don't ever want to hear about her, ever, never. All she ever did was give in to my dad. Shit, he beat me, and she stood there and let him." He banged the table with his fist. "And him, he was a mother-fucking bastard. I'm glad the son of a bitch is dead. He was the most evil piece of shit on this earth."

I dared to ask, "Did you kill him?"

"No, but I wish I had. The pleasure of watching him die would have been fantastic. He was a sick son of a bitch. My favorite memory of him, the one I truly enjoy, is of the day I was finally big enough to fight back."

Suddenly the hands were still. His fists clenched. His leg didn't move. He spoke harshly. "I waited for years, silently. I knew some day I'd be big enough and strong enough. Then one day when I was a freshman he came after me for no reason. He walked into my room. He never said a word. He ripped my posters off the wall. He smashed all the models I'd built since I was a kid. I went crazy. He was big, but neither of us realized how big I'd gotten. Every time I landed a punch it felt incredibly good. When the blood started from his nose, he went nuts, but I'd never felt such power. I beat him until he was on the ground beneath me. He bellowed at me and tried to hit back. I felt invulnerable. My mom screamed from my bedroom doorway. I remember Keith yelling, 'Don't kill him, don't kill him.' I only stopped when Keith tackled me off from on top of my god-damn dad, or I probably would have killed him." His breathing was rapid and fierce as the emotion and memory gripped him. "That night had one major effect. He never touched me again. We never discussed what happened. I never found out what set him off. Fifteen years of hell ended in less than five minutes. Do you blame me for being glad he's dead?"

I waited for him to bring himself under control. His ragged breathing slowly eased. I said, "No, I don't blame you for how you feel about your dad, Phil. But your mom?"

He slammed his hands on the table, "No way, man. No guilt there. She could have put a stop to that bastard any time. Do you know what my earliest memory of him is?" He looked from one to the other of us.

We shook our heads.

"Most people's early memories are of warmth and caring. The earliest thing I remember is pain and me crying, and this man screaming at me. I must have been three or four years old at the most." His voice dropped to a whisper. "I was too little to have done something that wrong." Tears started down his face. "How could she not have protected me? What kind of mom was she?" He cried quietly for a moment, then it was too much for him. He buried his head in his arms on the table and sobbed.

I hesitated a moment then moved over to the other side of the booth next to him. I put my arm around his shoulder. I made the sounds one makes at such times, hoping they're soothing and the right thing to say. He shifted and put his head on my shoulder and bawled. I held him tightly and rubbed the back of his neck and head.

A few minutes later his sobs slowed. I looked at Scott. Then I gave the two at the counter a quick look. Daphne had a restraining hand on the manager's arm. She shook her head at him.

When the sobs quieted to sniffles, I said, "Your mom is a

frightened woman, a very human person who made a mistake and didn't know how to correct it." He kept his head on my shoulder. The crying was softer now.

"She loves you, Phil," I said.

He sat up, took out a hanky, and blew his nose. He looked like the bewildered and frightened human being he was.

"You're going to be okay, Phil," I said.

"Yeah." He sniffed heroically. Tears stained the sleeves of his suit coat. "I'm a mess." His handsome grin flashed briefly.

Minutes later I judged him sufficiently pulled together to answer a few questions.

"Where are you staying, Phil?" I asked.

"With a friend. He takes good care of me."

"I really wish you'd consider coming back with us. Life at home could be worked out."

He shook his head. "No way."

"If we needed to talk to you it might help if we knew where to find you."

He wiped his nose, shook his head. "I can't tell you who I'm staying with. He told me not to tell anyone. He doesn't even know I'm meeting you. If you need to see me, check with Daphne. She'll know where to call."

"All right," I agreed reluctantly. "Phil, I'd like to check a couple things about your dad's murder. Scott and I want to find out who killed him. Since the body was in my classroom I'm a suspect. As you might guess, the police have been trying to find you. Because you disappeared, I imagine they think you had something to do with it."

"I was at Daphne's that night."

The answer was too quick, too pat.

He continued. "It was a slow night. I didn't turn a trick. I was 'against the wall' most of the night."

I thought of a dozen moral, psychic, and physical warnings that I didn't think he would listen to.

He added, "Daphne's my witness."

I was sure she would be. I asked, "Daphne's not worried about under-age prostitution and drinking?"

He shrugged. "I've been going there for a year. I get no hassles. She says I'm good for business."

I let the subject drop. "What time did you go home?"

"After closing, around four-thirty. I stayed to help them clean up."

"Were you out late often on nights you had school the next day?"

"Sometimes, not a lot. Depended on what mood I was in."

"Your parents never said anything when you came in that late?" I asked.

"They gave up waiting up for me years ago. My hours are never mentioned."

"Isn't it dangerous being a hustler nowadays?" Scott asked.

"No, I'm real careful. If a customer won't use a rubber, then it's no sale."

I resumed my questioning. "When you got home did you notice anything unusual?"

"Nope, as far as I knew everybody was in bed where they belonged."

"Wouldn't your mother have been worried if your dad wasn't home?"

"Maybe, but he kept odd hours a lot."

"Do you know where he went those odd hours?"

"No. He did it fairly often. Maybe once or twice a week. Nothing was ever said about it when I was around."

"Do you know of any connection between your dad and the Adonis-at-Large escort service?"

He looked surprised for a moment but all he said was no. I

wondered what was behind the surprise. His no sounded wrong to me. I moved on to my next question. "Do you think your mom killed him?"

He contemplated this seriously. "I'd say no. She was too scared of him."

"Outside the family, who hated him enough to kill him?"

"Anybody who knew him" was his instant response.

I tried again. "Was there somebody with an extra-special grudge, or who had a recent fight with him, especially at work? Think first before you answer."

"No—" he started to answer quickly, then hesitated. "Well, wait, a couple times he talked about Mr. Vance, the head of the department. He thought Mr. Vance was incredibly stupid. He used to make lots of calls trying to get people to support him against Vance at department meetings. I remember the second Wednesday of every month he shouted on the phone for hours. The meetings were always the next day. I tried to be out those nights."

"But other than Vance, there was nobody in particular who stands out in your mind, maybe even a friend in the department?"

"Nobody, he had no friends."

"This is a tough question, Phil, but I need to ask. I've heard rumors since the murder that your dad had sex with some girls in his classes in exchange for better grades."

"It's not a rumor," Phil said. "It's true."

His instant confirmation surprised me.

Scott asked, "Didn't it bother you?"

"No, by the time I found out, I already knew he was slime."

"How did you find out?" I asked.

"Greg told me."

"Greg?" was my one-word question.

"Yeah, let me tell you what happened. One night when we were sophomores, we were on our way to a basketball game. Greg forgot his letterman's jacket or some stupid thing. So we went back to his house. I waited in the car while he ran in. He was gone a long time. Finally he came back without the jacket. He was real pale. All night he was real quiet. I teased him about it. He told me to lay off. I was supposed to sleep over at his house that night. When we got back after the game he stopped me outside on the lawn. He took a long time about it, but he finally told.

"Greg found his older sister and my dad in her bedroom. Greg went in there thinking she ripped off his jacket. She did that to annoy him sometimes. According to Greg, they were going at it hot and heavy. That's why they didn't hear him. His sister begged him not to tell. Later she told him about the deal for better grades. She was a senior and needed to graduate. She gets mostly D's and F's like Greg and me.

"My dad threatened him, said he knew the computer access codes, and he could lower Greg's grades if he said anything. For whatever reason, Greg agreed to keep his mouth shut. I was glad he told me. I couldn't tell anyone because of my promise. Besides, his sister was always good to me. She and I even did it once when I was in the seventh grade and she was a freshman. Anyway, I guess it doesn't hurt to break my promise because now my dad's dead."

Scott said, "You and your dad made it with the same girl?"

Phil looked at him in total innocence. "She and I were little kids. It was no big deal."

I put my hand on Scott's arm to forestall another comment.

I asked, "Was Greg angry at your dad?"

"He was real mad that night. Kind of stunned and shocked too. It took him awhile, but he got over it. Now he and his sister are real good friends. Besides, Greg learned stuff pretty early. His mom and dad divorced years ago. Greg had sex for the first time in sixth grade. I know it's true because I had sex with the same girl in eighth grade and asked her."

"I can't believe kids have sex in sixth grade," Scott said.

"Mr. Carpenter, most adults wouldn't believe the amount of stuff we do. They're all working, and we have plenty of time after school to do whatever we want. Guys like me and Greg get lots of offers."

Scott raised a doubting eyebrow.

"Things have changed since you were a kid," Phil said.

"I was terminally shy at that age," Scott remarked.

I asked, "Do you know for sure if your dad did this with other girls?"

"Not for sure, but my guess is that he did. He was scum."

"I'll need to talk to Greg again," I said. "Can I tell him you told me all this?"

He thought about this a long time. Finally he said, "Sure, go ahead. Tell him I told you. He'll understand."

I wasn't sure there was anything more to ask. "How about in general?" I asked. "Was there anything else about your father recently that was out of the ordinary?"

"Jeez, it's hard to say. I haven't been around that much. I've been into hustling pretty heavy."

"Anything at all, any changes?"

"No," he said slowly, concentrating, then his face brightened. "He did seem stuck for money lately."

"How do you mean stuck?"

"Broke. There were times when he had tons of money. Lately he'd been screaming at the kids a lot. That's how I knew he was down on money."

"Do you know why he was broke?"

"Nope, can't help you there."

I'd asked all I could think of. I said, "Keith misses you a lot."

"He's a great kid. He's the only one I miss. I hated leaving him, but with Dad gone he'll be okay. I promised I'd get back to him. That's one reason I wanted to see you. Could you take him a message for me?" He took a long white envelope from inside his suit coat and handed it to me. It had Keith's name printed in block letters over the sealed flap.

"I'll deliver it, I promise," I said.

"Thanks." He hesitated, looked toward Daphne. "I should be going. We're going to a concert tonight. That's why I'm dressed up."

"Wait, Phil, there's one more thing I don't understand.

Why did you leave home? With your father dead wouldn't life there be easier?"

"It's time for me to make a break, Mr. Mason. I got a solid offer from somebody I trust. I hate that house and all my memories from it."

"What about graduating?"

"I'll handle that later. School's not important." He pointed at himself. "I've got my most marketable asset with me at all times, and I intend to make the most of it while I can." When we didn't say anything to this he said, "Look, I appreciate you looking for me and all, but I'm okay, really."

I wished I could believe him. I was afraid what he was into was way over his head.

"If that's all, I've really got to go. I've told you all I know. I hope it helps you find out who did it." He stood up.

"One more thing," I said.

"That's what you said a minute ago." But he smiled as he spoke.

"Do you know where your dad was that night?"

"No, sorry." He began to move away.

I gave it one last try. "Phil, you don't have to go back to where you're living."

He gave us his dazzling smile. "I want to," he said simply. He gave a little wave. "Nice to meet you, Mr. Carpenter. See you, Mr. Mason."

We stood up also. Daphne lumbered over. "You two wait," she ordered. The manager let Phil out the door. Without looking back, the boy crossed Wacker Drive and disappeared around the corner of the Sears Tower.

"He's really not a bad kid," I mused aloud.

Daphne raised an eyebrow at me. "I suppose you're right," she said.

"The man he's staying with, is he trustable? Will Phil be okay?" I asked.

"Yes. Certainly better than he ever was at home," she answered.

Scott moved to confront her. "At least at home they weren't peddling kids."

She shook her finger in his face. "Don't you throw that family bullshit at me."

Scott grabbed her arm. "You're turning kids into whores." His deep voice achieved its angriest rumble.

The manager made a threatening move, but this time Daphne wrenched her arm out of Scott's grip. She didn't retreat though. She thrust her face at his, her nose landing an inch from his chin. She shook all over and bellowed back, "Watch it, asshole. You've touched me for the last time."

Lowering her voice, but with her frame still trembling, she went on. "Let me tell you something, fuck face. I find these kids. I make sure they don't starve. I make sure they have a place to stay. I keep them away from rough customers. I make sure they're taught safe sex."

She backed away from him half an inch. "I care for these kids. That boy needed help. I brought him here tonight because I knew he needed to get some shit out of his system. He wouldn't talk to me. He wouldn't talk to his hustler buddies. There was no one else. He had to talk to somebody. He was completely torn up inside." She whirled away from him and stomped up to me. "And let's not get the idea that I'm a lesbian with a heart of gold. I also keep these boys around because it's good for business, very good indeed. They keep customers coming in the door at an enormous profit a year. Is it wrong?"

She answered her own question. "I suppose it is, but you tell that to some starving, shivering fifteen-year-old with no place to go. Am I supposed to send them home? Most don't have a home to go to, or not one they're welcome in. As you well know, many parents can't handle it if they find out their teenage darling is a cock sucker."

She plunked onto a counter stool, cupped her chin in one hand, and drummed her fingers on the pale-green Formica.

I was curious. I said, "I've been told the other gay bar owners don't like you."

She looked up at me. "That's right."

"Why not?"

"I'm sure you've heard reasons."

"But I haven't heard your side."

She eyed me thoughtfully. She motioned to the manager. "You can go, Derek." He let himself out.

"I own the franchise here," she said. "I've made some good investments. In two years I'll be a millionaire." She got up and began pacing the floor. "First, they don't like me because I'm a woman. Second, they don't like it that my place makes more money than any other gay bar in the city. Third, I don't get caught. I think they hate that most of all."

She stopped pacing, gave me a sly wink. "I have no intention of revealing that secret, now or ever."

She resumed her journey in front of the counter. "They probably told you I double cross them, that I won't go along, that I don't support the community unity. Those hypocritical bastards. They unite when they're scared. They've stabbed each other in the back a thousand times. Then when some straight politician smiles at them, they scramble like mad to do the bidding of their 'friend.'"

The pacing stopped again. "Let me tell you, there is no such thing as a 'friend' of the gay community among straight politicians. We've had so-called *friends* in this city for years. They've taken our support, our money, our votes, and what do we have to show for it?" She gave another bitter laugh. "Look how they've handled the gay rights ordinance."

She grabbed her coat from a nearby booth. As she buttoned it she added in a very quiet voice, "I know I'm exaggerating. They aren't all like that. But I get so sick of the snotty few who think they run this community."

She swept toward the door. "Fuck 'em all," she said as she passed us. "Let's go, boys."

We moved quickly as she held the door for us.

I tried to thank her as we waited for a cab.

"Save it," she said. "Don't bother me any more, and don't come in my bar again. That'll be thanks enough." She squeezed into a cab.

*   *   *

"She's an unbelievable woman," Scott said.

It was several hours later. We'd eaten dinner at Jerome's, one of our favorite restaurants. We were relaxing in Scott's living room in front of the fireplace. I'd built a fire. He sat up against a couch. I had my head in his lap, my feet rested on a low pile of cushions. As we talked he outlined the curves and valley of my face with his fingertips.

"I have mixed feelings about her," I said. "I think she's exaggerating about the bar owners. The ones I've met are decent people, trying to make a living like the rest of us. I don't agree with what she's doing with those kids, but I understand her reasons. Society will never take care of those boys. She's better than nothing, I guess." I sighed. "I do know that if I'm ever in a fight, I definitely want Daphne on my side."

I shut my eyes. I felt his fingertips feather over my eyelids.

Scott said, "I wonder if we can trust everything Phil told us."

"His answers were a little evasive on a couple of points"—I opened my eyes—"but overall I think we can trust him."

"Can you believe they both had sex with Greg's sister?"

"I don't want to think about that part. The kid's had an incredible life."

"Are you going to open the envelope Phil gave you?"

"No."

"It could be information about his whereabouts."

"He gave it to me because he trusted me. I'm going to deliver it intact. I will ask Keith if he'll let me see the contents, but that's all."

"I suppose you're right. Jim Evans must've been a sick man. I haven't heard one person say anything good about him."

"Yeah. Nobody we talked to is sad he's dead. I'll need to talk to Greg tomorrow. He wasn't very truthful last time. Greg may know more than he told Phil. You know, another thing Phil said made me think."

"What's that?"

"Maybe somebody else walked in on Evans while he molested their daughter. Some father or mother he couldn't bully into silence. Some parent angry enough to kill."

"That's real possible," Scott said.

"I'm going to try Meg to find out more about the father's money situation. She mentioned it when I talked to her. I wonder where the money came from. If at times he had a lot more, I wonder if he tried to rip off the school."

"You think that's possible?"

"He had to get the money somewhere. I'm also going to do the obvious. When we stop at the Evanses' house to deliver Phil's message, I want to ask Mrs. Evans if she knows anything. I doubt she will."

"Are you going to tell her we saw Phil?"

"I think so. That was the original point of this whole thing. It's almost impossible not to. If we're there to give Keith a message, the lies could get too elaborate. Keith might slip and tell her anyway."

"What if she tells the police? They'll be pissed you didn't tell them."

"Let's hope the police never find out. I'll have to think about what to tell them and how to handle it—if we decide to tell them. You're right though. They won't like it that we talked to Phil and didn't let them in on it. I don't want to be around when Robertson finds out."

We fell silent. He continued his caresses. I began to feel drowsy. "We should get to bed," I muttered.

He leaned down and kissed me. We went to bed, but not directly to sleep.

*   *   *

Scott drove me to school. He promised to pick me up at five o'clock for the trip to the Evanses' house.

At noon I sought out Meg. After leaving a parent volunteer in charge, we entered her office.

"How's the investigation going?" she asked.

"We found Phil."

"Is he all right?"

"As far as I could tell. But we couldn't convince him to come back."

"That's rough. Do the police know?"

"Not yet."

"Be careful. They could become nasty."

I told her what we learned from Phil. Her eyes blazed when I told her about Evans's relations with students.

"That son of a bitch," she said.

"I know," I said. "I wanted to ask you about the money situation again. Phil confirmed what you said about the swings back and forth. He said his dad was strapped for money lately. Had you heard anything about recent financial problems?"

"No word on lack of money. Doesn't mean he wasn't though. Phil didn't know why he was broke?"

"He said he didn't. I believe him. I wonder why it kept going up and down. There aren't a lot of ways for teachers on the job to make or lose lots of money."

Meg said, "As for extra money, I know he didn't have an outside job. And he didn't pick up any new extracurricular duties this year, I don't think. Let me check. I've got a master schedule here somewhere." She rummaged quickly through her files, pulled out a salmon-colored form. She ran her eyes down the list. "Nope, he isn't down for any of them."

"How would he lose money?"

"I don't know," she answered.

"Or how would he gain it?"

"That's just as tough. In a school there are very few ways to pocket cash. Oh, you can skim tiny bits of money here and there. Steal a pencil, or a paper clip for instance, but I don't see anyone with an illicit black market in Magic Markers. Makes no sense, there's no real profit in it."

"You're right," I said.

"You know," she said thoughtfully, "I've heard where you can skim money from athletic events. There was some scandal about that a few years ago in some northwest suburb."

"How does that work?"

"I can't swear to this, but I think I remember it right. You make sure you're the one to count the money after a sporting event. You underreport the size of the crowd and skim a bundle off the top."

"Don't they have people checking?"

"You would think so. I have no idea how our system works here, who counts it, who checks the counters. As far as I know, Evans had absolutely nothing to do with any part of the athletic program." She perused the master schedule. "He has no coaching responsibilities listed here."

"It doesn't sound promising, but I'll have to check it out later." I felt discouraged. "Is there any other way he could get cash around here?"

"Not that I can think of. There simply aren't that many opportunities in a school for significant stealing."

It had to be something outside school. The chances of my discovering what were dim.

Meg fiddled with a deck of cards on her desk.

"Catch those today?" I asked.

"Yes, you should see the collection I've built over the years. I could keep Las Vegas supplied into the next century." She gave an uncharacteristic yelp. "That's it!" she exclaimed.

"What is?"

"Gambling."

"Evans gambled?" I gave her a doubting look.

"It's quite possible."

"At school?"

"You're so naive. The math department for years has run a gambling operation. They set up a system on one of their computers. I hear it's quite sophisticated. If it's a sports statistic, it's in their program. They have it figured for every sport in every season."

"Do they bet significant amounts of money?"

"I don't know. I always figured it was small time. You'll have to ask them."

"How did you find out about it?"

"How do I find anything out? I listen."

"Could Evans have been involved heavily enough to make and lose large sums?"

"That could solve the riddle of the wild swings in cash he had."

"It's definitely something worth exploring. I'll talk to Vance again."

She glanced into the library. "Sorry to rush you, but Sylvester's out in the hall. I'll keep thinking and let you know if I come up with anything else."

"Thanks, you've been a big help."

We left her office. Sylvester stood by the desk talking to the parent volunteer. He eyed us suspiciously. Without skipping a beat Meg picked up a stack of nearby books, handed them to me, and said, "Here are the books of plays you requested for your script-writing unit. I'm glad we could help you."

I thanked her again and left.

After school I asked one of the other teachers to check in on my tutoring students. I didn't think they'd tear the place apart, but I like to be safe and know there's an adult nearby. I gave them their assignments for the hour. Then I took Greg aside and asked him not to leave even if I didn't get back by the end of the session.

I found Leonard Vance in his classroom.

"How're you doing, Sherlock?" He gave me a friendly grin.

"Hot on the trail," I said. "Can I check something with you?"

"Sure."

"It seems that Evans was pretty broke lately. I'm trying to find out if it's true and, if so, to track down the reason. Supposedly at other times he had vast excesses of money."

Vance sat down at his desk. He rubbed his hand across his chin. "Broke, huh. I'm not sure about that. Excess I am sure about. He used to brag about all the things he bought— fabulous stereo systems, new cars."

I didn't know how to put this delicately so I said, "Could he have made or lost a bundle on the gambling operation the math department runs?"

Instead of taking offense, he gave this idea calm consideration. He pressed his hands against the top of his desk and leaned forward. "I'd say no. I'd have to check the computer records to be sure. We keep close track of everybody's bets, winnings and losings. Individuals seldom win or lose significant amounts of money. Over a year's time a person might average a total winning of maybe five hundred dollars, tops. Nobody's ever lost more than two or three hundred in a year."

"Exactly how much money are we talking about, if it's not out of line for me to ask?"

"It's okay. We average about five thousand a week in bets."

"Five thousand?"

"That surprises you?"

"Yeah."

"It shouldn't. That's peanuts compared to most operations. Remember that five thousand is collectively. We have fifty or sixty people in the pool on a regular basis, sometimes over five hundred on big games or events like the Super Bowl or World Series. There's more than just the people at school in on it."

"Could somebody lose a lot, say if you backed losers for several weeks in a row?"

"With the whole system computerized we've minimized the risks. It would be a bad week if someone lost even a hundred. Usually we break even or win a little. Right here in the department we don't bet ridiculous amounts. We're teachers, remember."

"Could Evans have been cheating some way to increase his take?"

"No. When we set up the system, we tried all the cheating methods we could think of, and built safeguards against them."

"Could he have used the information from here to place side bets with another operation?"

"Sure, but we wouldn't know about it."

"Could he have duplicated your system and tried to set himself up in his own business?"

"He couldn't have an exact duplicate of ours. The discs we use can't be copied. He could set up one of his own, but that's a tremendous amount of work for one person. We have several people for each sport collecting and entering the data."

I strolled to the window. Outside the football team practiced in the November gloom. I turned back to him. "But he could have set one up for himself?"

"It's possible."

"But not probable."

"Right."

"And he couldn't be cheating?"

"No way."

I'd found out all I could. I prepared to leave. "One last thing I can't resist asking: Aren't you guys afraid of getting caught for illegal gambling or betting on school property?"

He gave a friendly grin. "Not really. Sure, people know about the operation, but we don't flaunt it. And what's to find as proof? A couple of floppy discs that are useless if you don't have the access codes. Significant dollar amounts change hands off school grounds."

In my classroom I found Greg's lean frame draped in the chair behind my desk. The other students were gone. He jumped up when he saw me.

"Is this going to take long, Mr. Mason? I've got to meet some guys in fifteen minutes."

"That depends on your answers, Greg."

"To what?" he asked.

"I talked to Phil last night."

"You did." His attempt at cool only partly covered his surprise. "How was he?"

"Fine, all things considered. He told us a couple things about his dad. Some were hard to believe."

"Phil can tell some pretty wild stories."

"He mentioned you several times."

"I never did anything."

"He didn't say you did. He talked about the time you guys stopped at your house before a basketball game, and who you discovered inside."

"Oh, shit," he whispered. He hung his head, stuffed his hands in his jeans pockets.

"I know this won't be easy to talk about, but it might help. It might be a starting point in finding out why Mr. Evans died, and who the killer is."

"I can't talk about this," he mumbled.

"Phil already told me. It's only a matter of time before the police find out and begin asking questions."

"Are you going to tell them?" His gaze remained fixed on the floor.

"I'd rather talk about it between ourselves." His shoulders lost some of their rigidity. "Greg, I don't want to bring trouble to you, your sister, or anybody else in your family. You realize if and when the police find out, they might try to connect Evans's sleeping around with students to the murder. They'd be dunces not to. Because of how angry you got that night they may begin to suspect you."

"Do you, Mr. Mason?"

"I think you're glad he's dead."

"You got that right," he said in a classic teenage mumble.

I ignored his comment. "But I don't think you killed him. I don't think you're the type, but the police might not agree with me."

"I was with friends the night he was killed."

"The police told us he'd only been dead a couple hours when I found him. He probably died around three or four in the morning. You mean to say on a night with school the next day you were out that late?"

"Maybe I did get home early," he admitted.

"Greg, let's make this easier. Help me. Can you tell me what other kids or parents might know about Evans's sexual activity? My guess is that someone else did the same thing you did; stumbled in on them, but that person decided to take matters in his or her own hands."

"I don't know of anybody," he said.

I couldn't tell if he was lying or not. I'd come back to it.

"A couple other things I need to know. You weren't entirely truthful the other day. You knew Phil was gay and hustling."

"Yes."

"Why not tell me this at the time?"

"You're an adult, Mr. Mason. I've never talked about sex with adults."

"How did your sister cope with you knowing about her and Mr. Evans?"

"I think I was more upset than she was. After the initial shock of me knowing wore off, as long as I didn't tell, she didn't seem to care."

I couldn't believe she would be that blasé about what happened. I wanted to talk to her.

"Did the two of you ever discuss the incident?"

"Yeah. She told me to stay out of her life. That if I told, she could tell some things about me. I'm no Mr. Perfect. I was past the tattle-tale stage anyway. My mom has enough hassles. There was no point in telling her. My sister and I were very close before that night. It took awhile, but we're friends now."

He looked at me, held his hand out as if for approval. "Was I wrong not to tell?"

"You didn't and it's over. It doesn't matter now." I thought for a minute then asked, "Greg, are you sure you don't know about anybody else having sex with Evans? Even the whisper of a rumor."

He stared back at the floor. "No," he mumbled.

"Greg, I need the truth."

His eyes met mine. "I ain't lying."

For the moment I believed him. I asked, "Do you know if that was your sister's first time with Mr. Evans?"

"I don't know."

"Did they do it again afterward?"

"I don't know."

"Where can I get in touch with your sister?"

"You're not going to talk to her?"

"I don't think there's much choice."

"She'll kill me for telling."

"You didn't have much choice about that. There are a lot of questions about Mr. Evans that people must have answers to. And remember Phil's really the one who told me first. You shouldn't have to worry."

"I hope not."

He gave me his sister's address and phone number. Finally he asked in a disgusted tone, "Can I go now?"

"Yes, that's all the questions." He hurried out.

Scott was in the parking lot when I walked out the door. On the way home I filled him in. Once there we did a quick workout then left for the Evanses' house. I'd found the address in the faculty list. As he drove I gave directions and finished my chronicle of the day's events.

"You know who I think is strange?" I said.

"Who?"

"This Vance guy."

"What about him? From what you said he's a pleasant, friendly, old codger."

"He makes me suspicious."

"We're suspicious of everybody, aren't we?"

"Yeah."

"I mean Mrs. Evans as wife is on the list on general principles. Both boys are, especially Phil. You don't trust the principal and superintendent. You didn't sound like you believe Greg told everything. Now you're suspicious of Vance. I guess we don't trust any of these people."

"Until we find the murderer everybody is a suspect, including the cooperative Mr. Vance."

"What's wrong with him?"

"Of all the people I've talked to he's the only one who knew Evans who didn't hate him."

Scott was quiet. We looked at each other. As we waited at a light I said, "Don't you find that odd?"

"I hadn't thought of it that way."

"If Evans was undercutting him constantly—"

Scott interrupted, "Not successfully, according to what Vance said."

"I have only his word for that," I replied.

"That's true."

"And I have only his word about the gambling operation. He could be covering for himself. Evans could have screwed it up in some major way, or he might have found a way to cheat them."

"Are you going to check it out?"

"I don't know anybody in the math department. Whoever I ask would be more likely to be loyal to Vance and not say anything. Certainly they would mention it to him. That could antagonize him, and I don't want that right now. The man could be hiding a lot. My original point stands. Why doesn't he hate Evans as everybody else does?"

"Maybe he's an easygoing type," Scott offered.

"Maybe he's a killer hiding a motive."

"Yeah, that too. Your list a minute ago didn't include the hordes who might have interrupted Evans in his illicit activities."

We talked over other aspects of the case the rest of the way but got no further with it.

The Evanses lived in Mokena. It was a small home with an attached garage. The gray house needed painting.

One of the girls answered the door. We asked to talk to her mom. Mrs. Evans came to the door smiling nervously and wiping her hands on paper toweling. She wore a pale-pink house dress, no makeup, no jewelry, and a worried look.

I introduced Scott, then asked her how she was. Before she could answer, Keith bounded down the stairs and into the room. He wore faded gray jeans and a number-34 football jersey. "Who's here?" he said. Then he noticed us. His face brightened when he saw Scott. "Hi, Mr. Carpenter, Mr. Mason." He turned to his mom. "Do you know who this is, Mom?" He blurted along without waiting for an answer, "This is Scott Carpenter. He plays—"

She interrupted. "You must be quieter, Keith. Don't rattle on like that. These gentlemen are here to talk about serious things. Go play downstairs."

"Can't I stay and listen?"

Mrs. Evans, with the paper toweling crumbling in her twitching fingers, tried to be severe. "Now, Keith, you know you can't stay around when adults have serious things to discuss."

"But I always do."

"No, you don't."

"I do too."

This type of domestic repartee irritates me. Scott rescued the situation. He said, "Keith, why don't you and I check out some of your stuff downstairs."

Keith jumped excitedly. "Yeah, I could show you my model planes. I've got the best collection in the world."

"Is that all right with you, Mrs. Evans?" Scott asked.

"He's being a pest. He knows better. Now, Keith—" Her voice lacked all authority. The fire and anger I'd seen the other night seemed to have deserted her.

Scott interrupted. "It's no trouble, Mrs. Evans. Tom can fill you in on everything. I'd like to see Keith's models."

He began to move toward Keith and out of the room. Mrs. Evans closed her mouth on any protest.

I handed Scott the envelope from Phil. "Why don't you take care of this?" I said. Scott took the envelope. The eager youngster led Scott away. In moments their voices drifted up from the basement.

She gave me a weak grin. "He's such a handful. His father was the only one who could control him."

We sat down on a pair of faded brown armchairs.

"We talked to Phil," I said.

Her hands fluttered to her throat. "Where is he?" she cried breathlessly.

"We talked, but we couldn't convince him to come back with us."

Her joyous look turned to confusion. "But why not?"

"He's a very confused young man."

"I'm his mother. I love him."

"I know that, Mrs. Evans," I said softly, "but I don't think he knows it."

"What does that mean?"

"He's been through a lot in eighteen years. The past week, to him, probably feels like a lifetime. He's on a roller-coaster ride. I imagine he thinks he can get off any time he wants. I hope he doesn't decide to do so at the top of a thousand-foot drop."

"He won't come home?" She pleaded with her look.

"Not yet."

Briefly she became fierce. "Where is he? I have a right to know. I want to talk to him."

"I don't know where he is," I said honestly.

"You found him once. How?" she demanded.

"By accident and luck."

"You're hiding him. You could lead me to him."

I met her eyes and held them. I said quietly, "I wish it was that easy."

The flash of fierceness in her eyes died. She leaned all the way back in her chair and shut her eyes. She seemed to have exhausted herself. At length she spoke. "Why try to fool myself? He hasn't needed his father or me for a long time." She paused. Finally when she looked at me and began to speak her voice was resigned. "Was he all right? Was he eating, staying someplace safe?"

"He seemed all right. By the way, that envelope I handed Scott was from Phil for Keith."

"He always tried to care for his little brother," she said. Her lips formed a bitter smile. She spoke more to herself. "When I was little I wanted a life like those on the TV shows, with mom at home, a kindly, wise, slightly befuddled husband, healthy, happy children, love." Her tone was wistful, almost a little girl's voice. She wiped her eyes with the remnants of the paper towel she still clutched and breathed deeply. "I guess I wasn't much of a mother. If I was, none of this would have happened."

"None of us has absolute control of our own lives, or of the lives of the people we love." I tried to speak words that would comfort her. "We aren't God. We'd like to be able to make everything right and perfect with a magic wand. We do our best. That's all anyone can expect of us."

She wiped at her eyes again and gave me a timid smile. "Thank you for your kind words." She paused. "I haven't thanked you for your kindness. I've been terribly rude. You found my son, and you took the trouble to come talk to me. I can never thank you enough."

I demurred gently then added, "Mrs. Evans, there was another reason we stopped by." I didn't know how to approach the subject delicately so I plunged straight in. "It's about your husband."

The worried look returned to her face. "Yes?"

"We were told his finances often fluctuated wildly and that he was short of money lately."

"Yes, that's true."

"Do you know why this was or how he worked the family budget?"

"No. I never had anything to do with family finances. He wouldn't let me. All he gave me was an allowance for household expenses. My husband's records are all here somewhere."

I wanted a look at that information. I asked her if I could see them. When she looked doubtful I said, "The information could point to the killer. If we discover who did it perhaps Phil will come home even sooner." It didn't make any difference if that logic was true, just if she believed it.

My last comment seemed to decide her. "I suppose," she said. She went to a beat-up old desk along the wall on the way to the kitchen. From one of the drawers she took various bank books and papers. She spread them on the desktop.

She said, "The police have gone over all of these. They didn't say they found anything unusual."

"They also didn't find Phil. Maybe I'll see something they missed." We stood at the desk and went over the records. Her ignorance appalled me. I suspected she'd never balanced a checkbook in her life, or even written a check.

What little there was to look at seemed perfectly normal. The statements were in order. The list of paychecks was meticulously accurate. The dates checked out with our paydays for the past few months. There were no unusual entries of money received. The payouts, too, were normal—ordinary household expenses for each month. We went through it all. At the end I was none the wiser.

"He didn't keep any other records?"

"No. He did everything on the computer upstairs. Then he brought the information down here and made entries."

"If he had computer records there might be more on them. Did he save those computer printouts?"

"No. At the end of the day he ripped them up into a million pieces."

"Could I see where he worked?"

She led me to an upstairs room. "This was his office at

home." She flicked on the light. The place was profoundly neat. Not a paper was out of place. All materials were in proper slots in exact parallels or at rigid right angles to each other.

"Did the police search in here?"

"Yes. They said they didn't find anything. My husband only kept school things here. The family things were all in the desk downstairs."

I walked around the room. There were two three-foot shelves filled with math texts and computer books. The computer sat on a gleaming steel desk. Next to it was a bin for floppy discs. It was empty.

"Were there discs in here?" I asked.

"There used to be. Someone broke in the day my husband was murdered. Whoever did it left a mess, but all they took were those computer discs."

"Do you know what was on the discs?"

"The police asked me that too. I only remember they were math games for his classes. I don't think the police spent much time in here. It's all school books and papers." She ran her hand along the book shelf. "I put everything back in order the way my husband kept it. I don't know why I did that."

"You're sure all they took were the discs."

"Oh, yes. I'd know if anything was missing. I dusted in here every day. Jim insisted on it."

Idly I ran my hand over the computer keys. Why would they take the discs? I wondered. For no good reason I flipped on the computer. I was surprised when a program began to appear on the screen. She moved across the room and joined me. "Has anyone turned this on since his death?" I asked.

"I haven't. The police might have."

"Or they simply didn't think there'd be a disc left in the drive. And who ever broke in didn't check it either."

The computer settled down to a sedate blink while asking for the user's identification code. "Mrs. Evans, do you know the access code?"

She gave a little-girl shrug. "No, I'm sorry."

I turned off the computer, flipped the lid on the disc drive, and took out the disc. It had no label or other identification markings. "May I take this with me?"

"I suppose, if the police . . ."

A loud crash and a resounding thump interrupted her doubts. There was a loud "oof," a brief silence, and then uproarious laughter.

5

Mrs. Evans rushed out of the room and down the stairs. I took the disc as I followed her out. I caught up with her on the landing overlooking the family room.

We saw Scott sprawled on the floor, and Keith draped over the back of a chair—both laughing uncontrollably. The two riotous ones below noticed their audience at the same moment. They pointed at each other and yelled simultaneously, "He did it." Their laughter redoubled.

I watched my lover laughing and pounding the floor like a little kid. It was impossible to keep a straight face. We joined the laughter. The two of them stopped only when they began to choke.

His mother descended the stairs and went to Keith. He waved her help away, and slowly composed himself. I looked around the room to find the debris from the crash. Nothing seemed broken or out of place.

"What happened, Keith?" Mrs. Evans said with a confused and, of course, worried smile. "Are you all right?"

"Yeah, Mom. I'm fine." He pointed at Scott. "Mr. Carpenter is funny. He can stand on his head and belch the alphabet."

We all looked at Scott, who now sat up in the middle of the floor grinning and holding his sides. This was the man who pitched no hitters in games five and seven of the World Series two years ago. That seventh game was the highest rated show in TV history.

Scott explained, "I got through the alphabet twice. Keith insisted I show him how. I was glad to. I helped him lean against the wall, with his legs up and all balanced. I was halfway through the alphabet again when Keith lost his balance. He fell into me. I fell into the bureau." He pointed at a piece of furniture now resting against the far wall. "The crash you heard was when it banged into the wall. I hope we didn't break anything." He picked himself up.

Mrs. Evans checked the bureau. "It's fine." She turned back to them. "You're not hurt?" she asked.

"No," they both replied.

She looked relieved.

"We're almost done with our talk," I said. "Is it safe to leave you two alone down here?"

They nodded, holding in grins that threatened to break out in renewed laughter.

"Why don't you show Mr. Carpenter one of your nice games?" Mrs. Evans suggested. "You could play quietly until we're finished."

"Okay," they said.

We went upstairs. Occasional laughter drifted from below.

"I hope your friend is all right," she said.

"He's pretty tough. I hope he didn't damage anything."

"No, and anyway the bureau is old. I am glad that Keith seems to like Mr. Carpenter."

"Yes, he does."

Her doubts about my taking the disc didn't resurface. I didn't remind her. I switched back to Mr. Evans. "About your husband."

The worried smile found its accustomed place.

"Do you have any idea where he went the night of the murder?"

"No."

I should have expected that by now. "What time did he leave the house?"

"Around nine."

"He didn't say anything?"

"No, he never did."

"Everybody else was home?"

"Oh, yes. I put the girls to bed right after he left. I looked in each of the boys' rooms at ten o'clock. They were watching TV."

"Phil said he was out all night."

"I don't know why he would say such a thing. If he was out, he left after ten, and I didn't know about it. I couldn't control what he did these past few years," she ended lamely.

There was nothing I could say to that. There was nothing more to learn from her.

In the car I gave Scott a long look. "You never told me you could belch the alphabet."

"While standing on my head," he reminded me.

"Yeah, that too."

"I don't tell you everything. There are still some mysteries about me."

He started the car.

"Do I want to know where you learned how to do it?"

"Sure. In the minor leagues. We used to do all kinds of

stupid stuff like that. There was never anything to do in the one-horse towns we played in. We didn't have any money to do it with if there was. So in cheap motels we entertained ourselves. One guy, Slimey Doubloon—"

I interrupted, "Slimey Doubloon?"

"He claimed that was his real name," Scott insisted.

"Okay," I said.

"Slimey was special. He could fart 'Dixie' after he ate a sixteen-inch pepperoni, sausage, and anchovy pizza."

"He ate the whole thing himself?"

"Had to, or he couldn't get beyond the first verse."

"Oh."

"Anyway, he was gross. And seventy-five pounds overweight but all muscle. If he ever hit the ball it went miles. Unfortunately, he spent most of his summers spinning wind. He couldn't learn to hit even a minor league curve." He paused.

"Is there more?"

"Sure. Slimey taught a bunch of us how to belch the alphabet."

"While standing on your heads."

"Right." He gave me his dazzling smile.

"You could have worked up a whole routine to entertain during the seventh-inning stretch."

"We did. We were set to do it for a July fourth game. Slimey'd already eaten the pizza for his part of the act. The management got wind of it the inning before and threatened to fire us all if we went on with it."

"Show biz lost a great act."

"Want me to teach you?"

"Thanks, I'll pass."

He drove for a minute in silence then asked. "Okay, Sherlock, what'd you learn?"

"The Evanses' marital relationship was straight out of the

Middle Ages." I explained about the finances. "If she knows anything about the murder, it's buried so deep I don't think anyone could dig it out."

"She's hopeless?"

"I think so. I did find one thing." I held up the floppy disc and explained, "If whoever broke in took only the discs, then there must be something important on them. They missed this one and it might be vital."

"Do you think you can break into it?"

"I doubt it, but I'll try some combinations. An access code like that could be anything. If he hid his true financial status on the disc, he probably made breaking into it supremely complicated."

"Oh."

"Or he could have made it as simple as using his name spelled backward. I'll work at it, but I don't hold out much hope for it. What did Keith say when you gave him the envelope?"

"He let me read the note. Phil talked about seeing him soon and to take it easy, that kind of stuff. Nothing helpful. He also included a thousand dollars."

"That's a hell of a scale he must be working at. I'd like to be in his union."

As we walked in the door at my place I heard the phone ringing. I hurried to snatch it up.

"Oh good, you're finally there," Meg said after she heard my voice.

"What's wrong?"

"I got a visit from Armstrong around five today. At first he tried to be all slick and friendly. What he really wanted to know was what you and I talked about earlier today."

"Sylvester must have reported seeing us talking."

"I assume so. I told him that as far as I knew my job description did not include revealing the contents of private conversations. After I said that, he switched to threats about fraternizing with faculty while working. I told him that as a librarian it was part of my job description to meet with teachers. After that he muttered threats about job security."

"I'm sorry to bring this pressure on you, Meg."

She laughed. "Don't be absurd. That son of a bitch can't touch me. I work because I enjoy it. I could have retired ages ago. I'm not worried. I called because he also made threats about you."

"What'd he say?"

"He said he knew you were pursuing the investigation contrary to his direct orders. That you were in big trouble, and that if I was part of helping you I would be in as much trouble. I'm afraid I didn't help the situation any by bursting into laughter when he said that."

I smiled at the picture of Meg laughing in Armstrong's face.

"You know how he splutters when he's angry?" Meg continued.

"I've heard, but I've never seen."

"He started doing that, spraying several shelves of nearby books. He listed more threats at the same time, and amid all those he let it slip that he will call you in for a meeting tomorrow. I thought I'd better warn you."

"Thanks. I'll be ready."

I started to apologize again, but she cut me off. "Nonsense, I enjoy this. You're doing the right thing, Tom."

I thanked her again. After I hung up I told Scott what Meg said.

"Can he do anything to you?" Scott sounded worried.

"He's the boss, not God. That's what administrators tend to forget. He's got no control over what I think—ever, nor over what I say and do outside of my classroom. None. Tomorrow he'll probably try to bully me into doing what he wants."

"That sounds like such bullshit to me," Scott said.

I shrugged. "What puzzles me is that so many administrators are former teachers. I've known some. As teachers they were relatively normal people. Giving them an administrative certificate turns them into arrogant, insensitive bullies. It's happened to every one that I know."

"Is that why you never became an administrator?"

"Partly, but the main reason I never wanted to be an administrator was kids."

He gave me a quizzical look.

I explained, "As far as I'm concerned there's no point in being in the education field if you aren't dealing directly with kids in the classroom. The vast majority of administrators have two main functions—push paper and punish kids. I can't see doing that with my life. The higher salary isn't worth the headaches."

We wandered into the kitchen to put together some dinner.

"What's in the fridge?" I asked as I looked through the cupboards.

Scott peered into the freezer compartment. He poked into it randomly. Bits of frost cascaded to the floor. "You haven't defrosted yet this year," he commented.

I defrost the freezer once a year. Someday I'm going to get one of the frost-free kind. That and the self-cleaning oven are probably the greatest inventions of the twentieth century.

He closed the freezer door.

"Nothing there?" I asked.

"Nothing visible" was his cryptic reply. He began rearranging items on the shelves. "There's a jar of olives here that look edible"—he sounded doubtful—"and some chicken that's been dead too long."

He doesn't criticize my food-keeping habits. He's just as bad. His advantage is he has the frost-free fridge and a self-cleaning oven.

I closed the last cupboard door. "Nothing up here."

"I suggest we eat out," Scott said.

Fortunately there was no other choice.

"Are we going to see Greg's sister tonight?" he asked as we got in the car.

"Yeah, let's. After we eat. She lives in Joliet. We can eat at Brun's in New Lenox. It's on the way."

As we drove I said, "What I don't get about Armstrong and Sylvester in all this is why they are so anxious to keep me from talking to people and asking questions. I don't buy that crap they gave me the day of the murder. I assume they have something to hide. I don't know what yet, but I intend to find out."

Greg's sister lived two blocks south of downtown Joliet. Even in the dark the neighborhood looked old and rundown. Her apartment was one-half of the third floor of what was once someone's sprawling upper-middle-class home. Domestic squallings leaked from behind sullen doors as we ascended the stairs. Brooding teenagers gathered in the pools of darkness of the stairwells.

When she answered our ring, she held a sleeping baby on her shoulder. She said, "Can I help you?"

I introduced myself and Scott.

"I remember your name from school, Mr. Mason. Come on in."

She closed the door. "I didn't catch your friend's name."

I repeated Scott's name. No reaction—she wasn't a fan. She had straight black hair and a pleasant face. She wore a faded gray dress and house slippers. I never had Sheila in class so I didn't know what she was like.

We entered what was now a living room. The walls were

bare. The only furniture was a couch and a lamp. Dust rose from the sofa as we sat on it.

"Let me put the baby down." She disappeared through a doorway. She came back minutes later carrying a beige folding chair. She set it up and sat down.

"This isn't about Greg, is it?" she asked.

"He's not in any trouble if that's what you mean," I answered. She looked relieved.

"It is about him in a way, though." Carefully I explained the situation to her starting with my discovering Evans's body last week. She listened without reacting. I concluded, "I hope you can give us some information that might lead to the killer."

She smiled slightly and said softly, "Phil should never have told, and Greg should have kept his mouth shut."

"Greg didn't have a lot of choice."

"Yes, he did. He should have denied it. It's none of your business." Her smile disappeared. Her voice remained low and flat as she went on. "I expect you want me to say this man traumatized me and lured me into evil beyond mention. Sorry, I can't help you there. I'd heard about his reputation from one of my girlfriends. Don't bother to ask who, I'm not like Greg, I won't be pressured into telling. After my girlfriend told me, I got interested. The boys who hung around us girls were so immature. I wanted to know what a real man felt like. I was far more willing than he was seducing."

"If not for yourself, think of the others who weren't willing. It must have been awful for them," I said.

"They aren't my problem. I knew what I wanted, went after it, and got it. And unlike my brother, I don't betray confidences."

I tried numerous other questions, but she refused to answer, finally retreating into stubborn silence.

Scott, seeing my growing frustration, forestalled my angry outburst by asking, "Won't you at least tell us what kind of person you think Evans was?"

She sneered at him.

I waited until my temper had eased enough for me to ask, "Do you know anything about a computer disc Evans had and why anyone would want to steal it?"

"No," she snapped.

Finally, a response. I tried a few more questions, but the stony silence returned.

I tried a last threat. "If we tell the police what we know they'll have questions to ask you."

She called my bluff. "Tell them. I couldn't care less." She stood up. "If that's all, gentlemen?"

"But you could help us find a killer," I said.

"I don't care. It's not my problem. To me Evans is just some guy who's dead."

There really was little else to say or do. We left.

"That was a bomb," I said as we started home.

"Yeah, but you've got another one to add to your list of people who knew him but didn't hate him." Scott paused then added, "How could she be that uncaring and unemotional about the death of someone she made love to? I know it was a couple years ago, but still something's not right there."

I agreed. "I'm not sure what it is. She was almost catatonic about the whole situation."

"I wonder how she pays the bills?" Scott asked.

"Me too," I said and added, "That was a bizarre experience."

Scott nodded. "Yeah, she was weird. Are you going to tell the police?"

"I don't know."

The next day at school started deceptively normal. The morning passed without a summons to the office. I'd about decided what he'd said to Meg was an idle threat when Georgette appeared at my classroom door. She beckoned me over.

"Mr. Sylvester wants you in his office," she whispered nervously.

"Someone has to stay with this class," I replied.

"I'm to stay with them." She looked petrified.

"They're only kids," I assured her.

"That's what I'm afraid of," she said.

Sylvester was in the outer office.

"You wanted to see me," I said.

He spoke stiffly. "Mr. Armstrong will speak to you in my office."

I went in. Sylvester closed the door behind me. He stayed outside.

Armstrong moved from behind Sylvester's desk. All of his fat friendliness from our first meeting was gone. Neither of us sat down.

"Well, Mr. Mason, you seem to have forgotten the directive we gave you in this office last week." Armstrong began to pace as he talked. "I thought you understood from our little chat that you weren't to speak to students and faculty about the incident, and you have."

He stopped and stared at me, seeming to expect an answer. I stared back. When I remained silent he resumed pacing. "You've questioned Mr. Vance several times. He's one of our finest teachers, head of one of our most successful departments, a prize-winning department. He's a loyal faculty member, not to be harassed by the likes of you."

I wondered if Vance told voluntarily or under pressure.

"Furthermore, you've spoken to current as well as former students, making all kinds of wild accusations about a man who can no longer defend himself."

I guessed that Sheila had called school and told about our visit. I wondered why. She didn't seem to fear any official involvement.

"How dare you talk to children who are incapable of dealing with such an issue. And I imagine you expected your little investigation to go unnoticed. It hasn't. I've been trying to get Detective Robertson on the phone. I'm sure he'll have a number of things to say to you about playing detective." He stopped in front of me, waving a finger in my face. "But worse for you, you crossed me, buddy, and you're going to pay."

He settled his bulk behind Sylvester's desk and stabbed a fat finger in my direction. "It would be far better for you if you turned in your resignation right now. In fact, if you resign in the next five minutes, I'll guarantee you a positive letter of recommendation from the district."

I sat down. "On precisely what in state law, school code, teacher contract, board policy, job description, or anything else do you choose to base this threat?"

"It's more than a threat, and I don't need any of those things. You disobeyed a direct order. That's insubordination. I don't need anything else but that."

"I have no intention of resigning," I replied. "If you wish to state your threat in front of my union representative and then follow proper dismissal procedures, go right ahead. I'd be delighted to have a formal hearing about all this."

He got pop-eyed with anger. He began to splutter. Sylvester's desktop received a heavy downpour. "Don't think I'm bluffing," he rasped.

"I don't care if you are," I said. He started to say something, but I stopped him. "What I would like to know is what you and Mr. Sylvester are trying to hide in all this?"

"We have nothing to hide," he snarled.

"I suspect you do, although I freely admit I can't prove it.

You've tried to keep a lid on me from the beginning and I wonder why."

"I told you we wanted to avoid scandalizing the public."

"I don't buy that crap. You don't work this hard at covering up if there isn't something to hide. This meeting confirms that. I think the police would find this very interesting."

"You bet they will," he said, "when they hear what you've done."

I shrugged unconcernedly.

He got a mean, piggy look on his face. Suddenly his tone shifted. He tried to mix menace with cruelty. "Well then, listen to this. If the police aren't enough to stop you, then maybe this will." He harumphed loudly then said, "If you don't resign now, I'll spread it all over this district that you're a faggot."

I raised an eyebrow at him quizzically.

"Don't think I won't. I know exactly which religious fundamentalist parents to call. It won't be me trying to get rid of you. It'll be community pressure that you won't be able to stop."

"Whatever you're hiding must be awful big for you to make threats that you think are enormous."

"I'm not bluffing," he said.

"Why did Sheila Davis call you?" I asked.

"I don't know any such person," he said quickly.

"What is it you've done, Mr. Armstrong? Molest children?"

"How dare you suggest such a thing?"

"Murder Evans yourself?"

He was inarticulate with spluttering. The desktop might float away if the deluge kept up.

"Rob the school district blind?" I added.

Flinging himself out of the chair, he leapt halfway across the desk at me. "Get out," he roared.

I remained seated. He looked like a beached whale. I enjoy it when administrators lose control.

Still leaning across the desk, he shook his fist at me. "I said get out," he bellowed.

"Sit down, Mr. Armstrong," I said.

He lowered his arm. His eyes blinked as if astonished to see me still there. He must be used to people cowering before his bullshit.

"Don't sit if you don't want," I said calmly. "You've made a mistake somewhere along the line. I don't know what it is. I doubt if you killed Evans. I suspect you made some slip-up and Evans caught you at it. Maybe he was a threat to you in some way, which would be typical of the man. You hoped with his death the threat would end. However, when they find the killer, or in the midst of the investigation, you're afraid it'll all come out. It would be best to tell the police yourself. Or if you want, tell me, and I could try to help."

He stood with his fist scrunched into the saliva on top of the desk staring at me. While I spoke he hadn't moved. He wasn't threatening or yelling now.

"Get out," he whispered.

I stood up. "I feel sorry for you," I said.

Outside my classroom, Georgette stood as far out in the hallway as she could while still keeping an eye on the room. I glanced inside. The kids talked quietly. "Did they behave?" I asked.

She took a handkerchief out of her sleeve and mopped sweat off her brow. "Yes, thank God. Some of them wanted to go to the bathroom." She added fiercely, "But I didn't let them."

"That's the spirit," I said. "We'll make a teacher out of you yet."

"Not me," she said, and left.

I resumed teaching. To me it was beyond obvious that Sylvester and Armstrong were up to their armpits in deep shit, somehow connected to Evans. Armstrong's threats I chose to ignore. He couldn't fire me for the bullshit reason he gave. As for trumpeting my gayness around—I'd long ago vowed I would never live in fear because of my sexual orientation. I doubted if he'd try that option. It would take too long to organize a campaign. If he did anything I suspected it would be to tattle to the cops.

Perhaps my calm reaction had blunted his bluster. If he was going to try something, there was no point in worrying about it.

When Scott picked me up that night, I told him what happened. I finished, "My guess is Sheila made it with Armstrong. That's the only reason I can think of for her to call."

"You're sure it was her?"

"Who else could it be?"

"You're right," he said.

"Are you worried about Armstrong's threats?" he asked.

"I don't think he can do anything to really harm me."

He looked at me as he waited for the lane to clear so he could pull into the driveway. "I sure hope not," he said.

I pointed toward the house. "We have visitors."

He followed my gaze to the police car sitting next to the house at the end of the fifty-foot drive.

The two cops who met us were very pleasant. They told us Detective Robertson wanted to talk to us. We weren't under arrest, but would we accompany them to the police station? They didn't know about what or wouldn't say. They were polite but firm. They said they would follow us in their car.

This visit to the police station was far more subdued than the last. There was only one person at the desk, a sergeant pecking at a typewriter. She ignored us.

One of the cops who'd been at the house led us down to a barren little room. It contained a table but no chairs. There were no outside windows, but along one wall was a mirror a fourth grader could guess had a viewing room behind it. Scott's first action was to wave through the mirror at whoever may have been watching. The cop told us to wait. We were left alone for over two hours. Neither of us said much. We waited in growing irritation. We'd had no dinner. Finally Scott said, "Maybe they intend to starve us into submission."

At that moment Robertson and Murphy walked in. Frank had a sour look on his face. Robertson was beet red and ready to explode.

Robertson started, "You two fucked me over the other night when I came over. I got suckered in by Mister Baseball Hero. Jesus, was I an asshole. Then he brings autographed baseballs for my boys. If it wouldn't break their hearts I'd throw them away when I got home. I may anyway."

Unwisely I asked what happened.

"You want to know? Let me tell you." His voice grew louder as he gathered steam. "You've talked to all kinds of innocent people and upset them no end. You tried to conduct official police business. You concealed knowledge from the police in a homicide investigation. You obstructed justice. You fucked up just about everything. I'll probably have you both arrested." He dropped his voice to a whisper. "Besides which, you lied to me."

"That we never did," I said.

He yelled, "You find a kid that half the police in the state are looking for and you let him get away. Not telling us is as good as a lie in my book." He slammed his fist on the table. "I hate liars."

"If we'd brought police we'd never have got to him."

"That wasn't your decision to make," Robertson snapped.

"You must have found out from Mrs. Evans," Scott said.

"No, it was the younger boy. He told us, or we still wouldn't know what you two were up to."

"Keith told?" Scott said.

"Oh, don't worry." Now he was loud and sarcastic. "He didn't turn you in. It slipped out when we went over there around three today for some regular checking. After the slip we got the story out of both of them. By four we were looking for you."

"Oh," I said. They must have just missed us at school.

"Yeah, oh. What if the older kid had gotten himself hurt or killed after you let him go? What if he killed his old man? What are you guys, God? One overpriced ballplayer and a nosy schoolteacher. Shit." His temper spent, he sat on the edge of the table with his back to us.

From near the door Frank said, "You should have told us, Tom." His voice was calm but reproving. We looked at him. Silence seeped into the tiny room.

"Do you want all we know?" Scott asked. I wished he hadn't.

"What for?" Robertson snapped. Silence descended, stretched.

Finally I asked, "What's going on here?"

"We arrested the murderer this afternoon," Frank said.

"You've kept us like this and you already had the killer." Now I was angry.

Robertson threw a snarl in our direction. "We wanted to finish up all the paperwork so we could bring a completed case to our amateur detective friends."

"Who did it?" Scott asked.

"Who killed Evans?" Robertson sounded insufferably smug and sarcastic. "We shouldn't have to tell you amateur geniuses."

Frank said, "Leonard Vance, the head of the department."

"He told me some negative things about Evans, but it never struck me that he hated him," I said.

"He may not have said anything to you, but he said enough to us. We have witnesses who say the departmental jealousy was incredibly fierce. It finally came to a head. We've talked to numerous school personnel who confirmed that they hated each other."

"That's not what he told me," I muttered.

Robertson heard. "That's why you should leave these things to the police. We know how to ask questions and get answers."

"Who told you they hated each other?" I asked.

"You're off the case," Robertson growled.

"At least tell me, did he confess?"

"No. He didn't need to. He has no alibi for the time of death."

Frank said, "It's safe to tell you that he was seen with Evans around midnight that night. He didn't deny that when we confronted him with it. He was the last to see him alive. We traced Evans's movements. At midnight he was in the Denny's restaurant in Orland Park with Vance. The waitress remembered them because of their loud arguing."

"How'd you trace them?" I asked.

Robertson said, "Solid police legwork. Following up leads and tips. Not running around like know-it-alls in over their heads."

I wouldn't have to practice to intensely dislike John Robertson.

"You're lucky," Frank said. "If Phil had been involved in the death, both of you would have been in big trouble. As it is the kid's simply a runaway. You're off the hook."

Their explanation didn't seem sufficient to me. But obviously no one wanted my opinion or intended to give a full account.

"Are we free to go?" I asked.

Frank said, "Only if you promise not to interfere in police business, now or ever."

"I don't want their promises," Robertson said, "I want

them scared." He turned to us. "Frank talked me out of arresting you guys. I almost did anyway, but I've got to work with the guy. If I ever see your faces around here again I'm arresting you. I don't care if you're here to pay a traffic ticket." He slammed the door as he walked out.

"Sorry, Frank," I said.

"Don't worry about it. You got in over your heads. Just let us do the police business from now on."

We went to eat at the Taco Bell on 159th Street. I know it's untrendy and probably even heretical, but I think their Mexican food is the best in the world.

We talked as we ate. I was pissed.

"Arresting Vance doesn't make sense to me," I said.

"Why not? You were suspicious of him."

"Yes, because he was the only one, until Sheila, who didn't hate Evans. It turns out he did, just like everybody else."

"Except Sheila."

"You know what really fries me?"

Scott pointed to the mess I had made eating a hard-shell taco. "That after over thirty years you still can't eat a taco without breaking the shell?"

I gave him a dirty look. I said, "It pisses me off that Robertson made us wait over two hours."

"That was a pisser," he agreed.

I took a bite and chewed for a while.

"They've got the wrong man," I stated.

He put down his burrito and gave me a steely-eyed look. He said, "Look, Tom, it turns out the guy had a motive. Plus he was seen with the victim. The police caught him. It's done."

I didn't want to give in. "Yeah, I guess," I muttered. We ate in silence for a minute. "I can't believe I fell for his lies."

"It happens. Forget it."

"I wonder which school personnel gave them the insight about departmental infighting. I'd lay bets it was Sylvester or Armstrong."

"You're prejudiced."

"And I wonder if the police found out about the gambling operation."

"If he didn't confess, maybe not."

"But someone in the department might have let it slip," I mused.

"Not if they were all in on it."

"If Vance killed him, why isn't the gambling part of the solution?" I said.

"I don't know." Scott sounded slightly frustrated. "We aren't in it anymore. We're out of it. It's solved."

"I've got my doubts."

"Come on, Tom, forget it. We almost got in a lot of trouble. Let's drop it, like the cop said."

"All right." I gave in reluctantly.

When I pulled into the driveway at my place I said, "It's supposed to snow tonight. I want to put the car in the garage." There's barely room for one person to walk around the car in the old farmhouse garage so I let Scott out first. He walked into the house while I pulled the car into the garage. I shut off the motor and the lights, took the keys and got out. I stretched in the narrow space. I was tired.

I closed the garage door. As I walked into the yard someone grabbed me violently from behind. A gloved hand clamped over my mouth kept me from calling out. My reactions weren't quick or strong enough to break the iron-hard grip.

"Mason?" a voice whispered.

I nodded my head half an inch.

"Keep your nose out of the Evans murder and forget about Phil Evans, or next time you'll get hurt worse than this."

Shattering pain thundered from the side of my head. Then nothing.

When I woke up I hurt. All over. Everything. I moaned.

"Tom." It was Scott.

I tried opening my eyes. I could tell it was night, but everything else was a blur. The effort to keep my eyes open was too great. I closed them. The gravel of the driveway poked into my back. I felt Scott's hands easing, caressing, his voice trying to soothe. "You're going to be all right. The ambulance is on the way." I felt a pressure on my forehead. I tried to pull away. Pain screamed in my head.

"Easy, I want to clean off some of the blood so I can see how bad it is." He tried to sound calm, but I detected the tremor of scared in his voice.

I groped for his touch. He took my hand. I put both of mine around his. I tried to concentrate on the warmth of his touch and not the pain in my head. I was only partially successful. I flickered in and out of consciousness.

Next I remember lights and movement. "Ambulance," I mumbled.

"I'm here, Tom." Scott's voice seemed to come from a vast distance. I realized I still clutched his hand.

The next time I woke up I was in a hospital bed. I felt drugged; probably, it dawned on me, because I was. The pain lived at the dull ebb of consciousness, gone for the moment.

I moved my head a quarter inch. It didn't hurt. Boldly I turned it more. I surveyed the room. The curtains were open. It was night. Scott sat in a chair, his head leaned to one side. He was asleep.

I tried to assess the damage. I flexed each arm. They moved slowly and stiffly. I brought a hand to my face. I touched an enormous bandage around my forehead. There was a small bandage over the bridge of my nose. I tried to look at it, became cross-eyed and then nauseous with the effort. A cluster of smaller bandages covered the right side of my face. Gingerly I continued inventory: ribs, legs, torso. There were sore spots everywhere, each earning a separate wince as I probed. Nothing obvious was broken—except my nose.

I realized I needed to piss. I was awake enough to decide to try the short trip on my own. I started to swing my legs out of the bed and almost passed out—obviously this was a mistake. Half off the bed, I lay back waiting for my equilibrium to return.

Scott rustled in his chair. He woke up and looked at me. He came over slowly and sleepily. "What the hell are you trying to do?"

"Practicing for a dance marathon," I grumbled.

He gave me a sour look then reached over and rearranged me in the bed.

"I gotta piss," I muttered.

He held a plastic bottle out to me.

I gave it a bleak stare. "No way. Help me up. I won't use that thing."

Scott sat on the edge of the bed. He yawned. "Don't be stubborn," he said.

"I'm not being stubborn," I said stubbornly. "I refuse to submit to the indignity of pissing into a bottle in a bed."

"I'll call the nurse, and we'll hold you down," he warned.

"Only if he's six foot eight and a redhead with a ten-inch dick."

"She is probably none of those."

"Shit. Come on, Scott, help me up."

"You'll probably fall flat on your ass and hurt yourself even worse. You're pretty banged up."

"I figured that out already. Now, help me up, please."

Reluctantly he helped me up. He was right. I shouldn't have tried it. It took fifteen minutes to make the fifteen-foot round trip. I managed it, barely.

I shut my eyes when I lay back down. I felt the pressure of his body as he sat down on the bed.

"Sorry now?" he said.

"A little." I concentrated on breathing evenly and fighting down the nausea. When my stomach was under control I opened my eyes and focused on him.

"Am I all right?" I asked.

"Pretty much. The doctor says your nose is broken, but fortunately nothing else. They aren't sure about internal injuries. They don't think so. In addition you've got lots of cuts and bruises, and maybe a slight concussion."

"I feel like shit." I paused and looked out the window again. "What time is it?"

"About four-thirty in the morning."

"What happened?" I asked.

"That's what I want to know," he said.

I told him what I remembered. "What brought you outside?"

"You took too long coming in. I got an uneasy feeling, so I came out with a flashlight and a baseball bat. I saw you on the ground with two guys kicking you. I went nuts. They tried to fight, but I landed solid hits with my first swings of the bat. They ran off. I'd have chased them, but I was worried about you. When I checked, you were unconscious, and there was a lot of blood. I called the ambulance and here we are."

I asked the obvious question. "Why warn me away? They arrested the killer. I don't get it."

"Maybe whoever it was didn't know they'd arrested the killer," he suggested.

"That happened hours before. If Vance is the killer you'd think they'd know what happened to him."

"Maybe they have lousy communications?"

"I don't think that makes sense."

"What 'they' are we talking about?"

"I don't know."

"Maybe the police arrested the wrong guy?"

"That makes a bunch more sense to me."

"And whoever did it wanted to warn you away?"

"We were close to something someone wanted to hide. Presumably the killer. Or maybe close to information that threatened somebody."

"You mean Sylvester and Armstrong."

"Yeah."

"I'm not sure that makes sense. Almost anybody could have attacked you."

"Only anybody who wants to keep us from looking into the murder."

"Then why not attack both of us?" Scott asked.

"Maybe they didn't want to try taking both of us on, or maybe they thought one warning would serve for the two of us."

"That reminds me, there were two cops here to ask questions. I couldn't tell them much because I didn't see a lot. They said they'd be around in the morning."

"Something to look forward to," I replied. I looked out the window. Framed in the light of the street lamp, the first flakes of the promised snow drifted lazily. I was exhausted and too tired to puzzle out the whos and whys. I closed my eyes and slept.

Frank Murphy arrived the next morning around eleven o'clock. I was awake and restless. I still hurt, but I was ready to go home. Scott insisted I wait for the doctor's approval. We talked to Murphy together.

"I didn't know they sent homicide detectives out on assault investigations," I said.

"Usually they don't, but I heard your name among this morning's reports. I thought I'd come check it out. What happened?"

When I finished he asked, "You didn't get a look at them?"

"Not at all."

"I did," Scott said, "but I didn't really see much. I dropped the flashlight when I attacked them. The lights from the house were dim. I couldn't even tell you if they were black or white."

Murphy turned back to me. "How about their voices?"

I said, "The voice that whispered was so low and gravelly, I couldn't tell if it was natural or disguised."

"They didn't say anything while we fought," Scott added.

"And you think it had something to do with your snooping around?"

"Don't you?"

"If Robertson was here he'd say no, and that you must have misunderstood what the attacker said."

"I didn't misunderstand," I said. "What other motive was there? I've still got my wallet and money. It wasn't robbery."

"Robertson would also say that random violence can strike any one of us anytime."

"But he's not here, so you think . . ." I let my comment dangle.

"I think it's real curious and more than a coincidence, but I don't pretend to be able to explain it. I believe we have the right man, but I'm open to exploring any options you can give me."

We told him the whole story—including the gambling, the sex with students—everything.

"How'd you get people to tell you all this?" was Frank's first reaction.

I tried to shrug casually, but it hurt too much. "Do you think anything we've told you will help?" I asked.

"I don't know. I have to be honest with you. Robertson, the lieutenant, and the state's attorney all think Vance did it. Interest in the sex charge would be minimal because Evans is dead. No one to prosecute, no headlines to grab. Furthermore, a lot of what you told me is unsubstantiated. If we send a cop to ask these same questions each person could simply deny it all."

"But there were two of us there most of the time," Scott protested. "I'm a witness."

"You aren't cops. You had no official status."

Scott swore. "Can't you do something?"

"I can talk to my superiors about reopening the case, but I don't hold out much hope."

"Could you at least tell me a couple things to satisfy my curiosity?" I asked.

He hesitated. "What do you want to know? And you haven't heard any of this from me."

"What does Vance say about them being together?"

"He says it was departmental business."

"At midnight? On a Wednesday?"

"He swore it was true. We asked him what business. He clammed up. The information on gambling you gave me might open him up."

"Let's say they did discuss gambling," I said. "Then they had a fight. Evans was a royal prick. I can easily see a major disagreement. But then what happened?"

"Vance says he went home, and he didn't know anything until the next morning. Obviously he didn't tell us about their meeting the first time we talked to him. That's what made us suspicious."

"Did he say why he didn't tell?"

"He didn't want to be implicated."

"And now he is." I shifted in the bed. "Did you search his place for the murder weapon?"

"We don't expect to find it. It's too easy to drop a heavy blunt instrument off a bridge, or in a distant trash can."

"How'd you know to question him again? Who let you know they were together?"

"The medical examiner found undigested food in his stomach. He concluded Evans had eaten within a half hour before he died. There aren't that many places open to eat around here at that hour during the week. We started asking around, showing his picture."

"He could have eaten in Chicago and driven here," I suggested.

"Or eaten at home or at a friend's," Scott added.

"Not in Chicago. It's an hour's drive. We knew he wasn't at home. He wasn't with anyone he knew, or at least any who would admit it. We decided on the possibility of a restaurant within the area. It was something we had to check. We'd gone to eight other places before this one. We had another ten to go within a fifteen-mile radius. It took awhile to get to everyone who worked that night at each restaurant. It turns out the waitress that served them had off all weekend. We talked to her Tuesday morning."

"She was sure it was Vance?"

"We matched the description she gave us with everybody connected with the case, including yours. She picked Vance's picture out right away."

"There wasn't some anonymous tip?" I asked.

"No. Nor any car chase, shootouts, tear gas, or machine guns. There seldom is." He smiled.

"What I mean," I said, "is it would make more sense to me if somehow Sylvester and Armstrong steered you to Vance."

"How so? You don't like them, but that doesn't make them conspirators in a murder."

"It's the type of thing they would try in order to divert suspicion from themselves."

"We did talk to them again yesterday at your school. In addition to telling us about your evil ways, they told us about the competition in the department. Did you know Evans was in line to be head of the department?"

"No," I admitted.

"He had seniority. Vance saw him as a rival."

"I don't buy that. Vance's job was secure."

"Maybe," Frank said. "What about this then? If what you told me is all true, wouldn't they try to divert the suspicion to you?"

"Probably," I said.

"They didn't. Sure they told us how rotten you are, but when we asked about Vance, they were most helpful. And besides, they had no way of knowing Vance and Evans met that night. I think those two are out of the picture."

"I can't believe that," I said.

"I do agree they've done something illegal." Frank added, "I just don't think whatever it is has anything to do with the murder."

"Maybe not," I said. I let it rest. I had no proof.

Frank said, "I'll want to see that computer disc. We might be able to get into the program."

"It's at home," I said.

"I'll send someone by to pick it up later," Frank said. "You can let the police handle it now."

After Frank left I said to Scott, "You need to go home and make a copy of the disc."

"If the police find out they'll be pissed."

I tried my most seductive smile on him. He held up his hand. "That doesn't work with your head all bandaged. Besides, you know that computer stuff baffles me. I'll never be able to make a copy."

"Oh, yes you will. You have to. If necessary you can call me from home and I'll guide you through it."

"Shouldn't I wait here for the doctor's report?"

"This is more important. I don't want the police to get there before we have time to make a copy. You've got the car keys. I can't leave without you. You could be back here in less than an hour, half an hour maybe. Then you can talk to the doctor to your heart's content."

He didn't like it, but he agreed. I explained to him what to do and he left.

One of the few things I let him buy me was the most up-to-date and sophisticated home computer system on the market. I'd worked on the Evans's disc in brief snatches since we got it. I'd had absolutely no success. Now I for sure wanted to keep a copy. It was the last fresh clue I had. Neither the killer nor the police would stop my investigation.

*　　　　　*　　　　　*

That afternoon the transfer from the hospital to home was smooth and easy. The doctor wanted to keep me another day. I convinced him Scott would take care of my every need.

At home Scott got me settled in and comfortable. He spent part of the afternoon installing the state-of-the-art security system he'd bought that morning. This time I didn't object.

He'd called in sick for me that morning. That night I

called Sylvester myself. I let him know I'd be out another day. Sylvester was subdued and businesslike. He did not wish me a speedy recovery.

A cop came by around four o'clock to pick up the computer disc. Earlier I'd checked the copy Scott made. It was perfect.

I spent the evening propped in a chair in front of the computer going through all the combinations I could think of to get into Evans's program. I had no more success than before.

I was still sore and tired from the beating so I went to bed early and slept late the next day. By now I was up and mobile, slow but active. I insisted Scott attend a luncheon he had scheduled and that he go to an afternoon photo session for the cover of some magazine. I worked all day at the computer, still no luck. Around eight Scott brought home dinner—take-out Chinese. Afterward I went back to the computer. He worked with me, offering suggestions. It was useless. None of it did any good.

We went to bed around ten-thirty. Scott gently massaged my various aches. I fell asleep wrapped in his arms.

Dim pounding nudged into my brain. I woke up. I glanced at the digital clock. It was 1:17 A.M. The pounding continued. I realized it was someone at the front door. I looked at Scott. He slept on. He claims he slept through a tornado once. I shook him. He mumbled. I hurried into some jeans. The doorbell began pealing spasmodically. I shook him again. "Wake up," I said. Scott became semiconscious. "Someone's at the door. It's one in the morning. I'm going to answer it."

I threw on a shirt and padded through the house. I didn't
turn on any lights. Carefully I peered around the curtains
that covered the picture window. I could make out a dim
figure on the front door step. I felt Scott glide up behind me.

"Big help your security system is," I muttered.

"It's designed for break-ins, not someone knocking on the
front door."

I opened the curtain wider to get a better look.

"Be careful," he warned, then whispered, "Can you see
who it is?"

"No," I whispered back. The person appeared small and
slight. "I think it's a kid." I paused. "Whoever it is is alone."

"There could be others hiding in the dark." Scott sounded
ominous. "Let's call the police."

"It's a kid alone. I'm sure of it." I walked to the panel of
switches for the outside lights and turned on the porch light.

The pounding and ringing stopped. Scott, in my place at the window, said, "It's Keith Evans."

Immediately I opened the door and let him in. Scott turned on the living-room lights. The kid looked awful. His hair was windblown and ragged. Mud covered his shoes and pants. His coat was torn. Even inside the house he shivered.

Without preliminaries Keith blurted out, "Phil called. He's in trouble. You've got to help."

I said, "Keith, start from the beginning and tell us what happened."

"A little before midnight the phone rang. It was Phil."

I interrupted, "Where was your mom?"

"I don't know. She left around ten-thirty tonight. She didn't say anything about where she was going or when she'd be home. She wasn't back when the call came, or when I left."

"Is that normal for her?" I asked.

"It was real strange."

"Weren't you worried when she didn't come home?"

"No"—he shrugged—"should I be?"

"I don't know," I said truthfully. This was a totally strange family. "What did Phil say?" I asked.

"He sounded real scared. He said to get to you, Mr. Mason. He said for you to come rescue him."

"Where was he?"

"He didn't get a chance to say. Right in the middle of a word the phone went dead. I'm scared, Mr. Mason. Where is he? Why is he in danger? What's going on?"

I ignored his questions for the moment and asked, "Why didn't you call us?"

"I looked on my dad's faculty list. Your address was there but not your phone number. I tried the operator, but you were unlisted. Phil said it was an emergency and not to call the police. He sounded bad. I figured I better talk to you right away. I looked at your address. It didn't seem that far, so I decided to walk it. It was a lot farther than I thought."

"How'd you get so dirty?" Scott asked.

"On the way here I kept tripping over stuff in the dark. I ran into fields or people's yards every time a car drove by because I didn't want somebody to report a kid walking around. I fell into the snow a couple times when I jumped off the road." The storm the morning before had left a couple-inch taste of winter.

"Why not wait for your mom?" Scott said.

"I was scared. I had to do something fast." Then he snorted contemptuously and looked away from us. "My mom can't do nothing. She's a wimp."

"Easy, Keith," I said, "she's your mom. You know we'll have to call her and tell her you're here."

He hung his head. I reached for the phone. He mumbled the number when I asked for it. It rang twelve times before one of the girls answered. I asked for Mrs. Evans. After a few minutes she came back and said her mom wasn't home. I explained who I was and the reason for my call. She remembered me from our visit. She spoke in a scared whisper, but seemed to understand what I wanted. She agreed to leave a note for her mom telling her where Keith was. I spent some time reassuring her. I urged her to go back to bed, which seemed fatuous, but I didn't know what else to say. Then I hung up, wondering where Mrs. Evans was. I decided I couldn't waste time worrying about her. The main problem was Phil. Where the hell was he?

I tried a few more questions on Keith. "Did you get any clue at all from what your brother said that might give a hint about where he was?"

Keith furrowed his brow and thought a minute. "I don't remember anything."

"If you could remember even a small detail," I said, "a

background noise, a conversation, a TV, a stereo, maybe even outdoor noises."

He thought again then said, "Sorry, nothing. Only his voice." He gave us a plaintive look. "Are you going to save him?"

"We don't know where he is," I said gently.

"You've got to help him, Mr. Mason. He's in danger."

I considered phoning the police. To them Phil was now only another runaway. Further, I had no specifics to tell them, only a cut-off phone conversation as told by a thirteen-year-old.

The only thing I could think of was Daphne's bar. I got the number from directory assistance and called. The noise on the other end was loud enough that Scott and Keith could hear it from where they sat. The Womb must have been in high gear. My normal tone of voice produced no response. I tried shouting into the phone. Whoever was on the other end couldn't hear me even then. I yelled that I wanted to talk to Daphne. My words echoed around the living room. On the other end the phone slammed down. I tried four more times with the same amount of success. Finally all I got was a busy signal. If we wanted to rescue Phil that night we'd have to drive down there and hope Daphne would talk. I told Scott. He agreed.

"Where're you going?" Keith asked.

"A place that might give us a clue to where Phil is," I said.

"I want to come," Keith said.

"It's not an appropriate place for a thirteen-year-old," Scott said.

"I want to come." Keith was stubborn.

Scott explained to Keith that it was too late for him to be up and out and that he needed to be in bed.

Keith remained adamant.

I decided the kid was in this deep enough and deserved a

full explanation. I expected he might not understand all of it. He might lose respect for his brother. I knew for sure I did not intend debating with a thirteen-year-old in the middle of the night. It wasn't up to me to protect the sacred familial sensibilities for him. Mr. and Mrs. Evans had destroyed them for Keith long ago.

We went to finish dressing. I explained my reasoning to Scott. He looked surprised, but thankfully didn't argue. I let Scott tell the kid of the change in plans.

Keith wore a shirt, pants, and socks of mine. The pants had to be rolled up a foot to keep him from tripping over the legs. A rope tied around the waist held them up. The shirt hung down to his knees. For a coat he wore my old marine jacket. In the car he sat between us. I explained everything I knew about Phil's situation to him.

He accepted it all silently. At the end his only question was "Because Phil's gay, does that mean I am?"

I told him no. Contented with that answer, he stared out the window at the passing lights. As we entered the Dan Ryan from I-57, I could see him desperately trying to stay awake.

By the time we exited the Lake Shore Drive on Fullerton his yawns came more frequently. It was a couple minutes before three. Keith stumbled out of the car after us when we parked. Scott started to protest, then swallowed it. Keith had seen this much, he might as well see the rest.

The bouncer at the door tried to stop us. "We're closed and you can't bring that kid in here," he barked.

Scott punched him. The guy plopped backward. Stunned, he sat shaking his head. We went in. The bar lights were up, revealing the scumminess the darkness usually concealed. Daphne stood in front of the bar counting money. She wore an acre of pink chiffon. She looked up. "Christ, you guys." Then she caught sight of Keith. "What the fuck is this? A clown act? Even I don't take them this young." She glared at me. "I told you before to stay away. I meant it. Get out."

The bouncer had recovered, and sidled up next to her. "Marvin, how'd you let these assholes in here?" she asked.

He rubbed his jaw where Scott hit him. He whined, "I tried to stop them, but they got rough."

"Clarence, come here," Daphne called. The bartender from the other night appeared from a back room. He propped himself on the other side of Daphne. She announced to us, "I want you out of here. You can leave by yourselves or we'll put you out. You have three seconds to decide."

"We need to find Phil," I said.

"He's not here. Get out."

"He's in trouble," Keith shouted.

"I don't care. Your three seconds are up. Dump them," she ordered, then added, "but go easy on the kid."

I planted my feet. Scott took a position next to me. "Daphne," I said, "I don't want a fight. We don't want trouble for you, but we stay until we get information."

"Do it now," she commanded. "Throw them out."

They came from opposite sides of the bar. They were bigger than Scott and I. The fight was brief. They were muscle-bound clods, more for decoration in scaring lonely old gay men than for real strength. Plus Scott and I, battered as I was, were in better shape than they. A moment later the two flunkies rested on the floor, one up against the bar, the other with a turned over table as a cushion for his head. Daphne didn't join in the brawl.

Scott and I breathed easily. My knuckles were sore, but that was all.

"Wow," Keith said, "you guys are great."

"Shit," Daphne said. "Fucking wimps."

For a minute I thought she might try attacking us herself. Shakily Clarence and Marvin pushed themselves off the floor. They eased slowly away from us. The fight was out of them.

"Should we call the police?" Marvin asked.

"No," she snapped. "You couldn't handle them so I'll have to." She continued to eye us warily for several moments. Finally she heaved her massive shoulders in a thunderous shrug. She waved the two of them away. She gave me a piercing look and said, "What am I supposed to be? Mother Theresa for that whole family? Yes, Phil was here tonight. He left around ten-thirty. I haven't seen him since. His mother was in about eleven-thirty looking for him."

"She was here?"

"That I wouldn't make up."

"How'd you know it was her?" I asked.

"Honey, this mousey suburban-looking woman walked in here. She took one look and freaked—like this was all the circles of hell at once. But she stayed—took a lot of guts. Mamma looking for her young, I guess. She asked a few people about Phil before I could get off the bar and get to her. Marvin should have stopped her at the door, but he's new and not too bright. Probably thought it was the latest drag fashion. She asked me if I knew where Phil was."

"Did you tell her?" I asked.

"No," she snarled. "I'm not here to play nursemaid to fucked-up families. She left abruptly and without learning anything."

"She wasn't home when we tried to call her a little while ago," I said.

"She didn't leave me her itinerary," Daphne responded.

"And you just threw her out," I said.

She stabbed a finger at me. "Look, buddy, I went out of my way to help you once. You've got all the nice you're going to get from me."

I explained about the phone call. "He could be in dangerous trouble," I concluded.

"Could be," she agreed.

"You helped us before," Scott said. "You knew how to get hold of him then. Why not help us?"

"Then and now are two different things," she said. "It's not worth my place here, or my living, to go further." Suddenly she looked annoyed with herself. "I've helped enough and I have work to do." She eyed me carefully, almost kindly, I thought. She said, "Why don't you get the hell out? Go back to your safe suburb. Forget Phil. He's where all lost pretty young boys go in this city. He'll be better off there."

Abruptly I said, "Let's go." Something she said had started me thinking.

In the car Scott asked, "Why'd we give up?"

"If we stayed a year we wouldn't get any more out of her," I said. "She let it slip that there was someone behind her. Someone who I think has a strong hold over her."

"Who?" Scott asked.

"I have no idea."

"What about Phil?" Keith asked.

"He wasn't there, obviously," I said, "and there was no way we could get the information out of them."

"Couldn't you guys beat them up and make them?" Keith asked.

I suppressed a smile. "We're not equipped for extensive torture," I told him. He subsided.

"What's next?" Scott asked.

I drove for a while in silence. The lights of the Loop glittered majestically as we drifted southward on Lake Shore Drives's new S curve. I waited until we drove past McCormick Place on to the Stevenson Expressway before I answered.

"I want to try and get into the computer program again. Something Daphne said gave me an idea."

"What'd she say?"

"Something about where all lost young boys go in this city.

And remember when we heard about the escort service that specializes in young guys?"

"But we got nowhere with that phone call. What would Jim Evans have to do with it anyway?"

"Maybe nothing. But what if there is a connection? Remember Neil said there was. If my idea doesn't work I haven't lost anything. If it does then I think we're a lot closer to catching the real murderer."

It was after four. Besides the lack of sleep I was still worn out from the beating. I noticed Keith. He'd fallen asleep while we were on Lake Shore Drive. He slept with his head resting peacefully on Scott's shoulder.

It was after five when we got home. Keith was sound asleep. Scott carried him into the house. He put him on the couch and covered him with a blanket. Keith stirred briefly then went back to sleep.

I called Mrs. Evans. She answered this time. She sounded exhausted but, even taking that into account, she seemed curiously uninterested in what I had to say about Keith and Phil. When I asked questions about her whereabouts, she was totally uncommunicative. I didn't pursue it. I planned to talk to her after school. I told her we'd be there at four-thirty. She dithered about it, but agreed when I pushed her.

Scott and I sat down at the computer. I inserted the disc, turned on the computer. We watched the preliminary data print on the screen. The question then appeared that I hadn't been able to get beyond for days. IDENTIFICATION CODE? The cursor blinked on and off waiting for my response. I typed in Adonis-at-Large. The screen cleared. The disc drive hummed. Then the three most dreaded words of the computer age flashed on the screen, FILE-NOT-FOUND.

I pounded the table softly. "Shit, I thought that was it."

Scott spoke comfortingly. "You've given it a good try."

I glanced out the window. The winter darkness held on. I

returned a baleful stare to the computer screen. I was depressed.

Scott rested a hand on my shoulder. "Maybe after you've had some sleep you can try again," he said.

I shook my head. "I'm not going to be able to sleep." I was angry and irritated, and worried about Phil. I thumped the computer screen with my finger. "I want to work at this a little longer."

"Okay," he said. "I'll make us some coffee."

I returned to the computer screen. I stared at the three little hyphenated words. There had to be some combination that worked to give me the information Evans had stored. In a mindless exercise I tried pressing one key at a time starting at the top. Maybe it was those words and a simple combination of keys. I must have been truly tired. If it was random, then my punching was hopeless.

I came to the caps lock key, and it dawned on me. I shouted in excitement. I also felt like a fool.

One of the simplest maneuvers and I missed it. They teach it to elementary school kids. If you type in your access code all in capital letters, you've got to type all capitals to retrieve it.

Scott appeared in the doorway. "What?" he asked.

"This has got to be it," I said. I typed in ADONIS-AT-LARGE. Once again the screen cleared. The disc drive whirred. Beautiful green letters began to dance across the screen.

"You got it!" Scott exclaimed.

It was all there: data from the gambling in the math department, records for Adonis-at-Large, even what Evans held over Armstrong and Sylvester's head. We studied the figures. It took almost an hour to go through it all. We went back over the high points.

"Vance lied. Evans ran the gambling operation. Maybe

Evans didn't control it at the beginning, but he did before he died." I tapped the computer screen. "Look at this."

A list of faculty members with the amounts owed Evans appeared, some as low as $50. Vance owed $9,500.

"Plenty enough to kill for," Scott commented.

"And maybe Evans was short this kind of money to someone else. And he may have had gambling debts of his own." The evidence for this was less clear. Someone owed somebody over $20,000. It had to be Evans. But who'd he owe it to?

We examined the records for Adonis-at-Large. Some listings were only names, but most included phone numbers, dollar amounts, and addresses or at least an indication of a region in the metropolitan area. All had listed their sexual interests.

"These are clients," I said. Under Southwest Suburbs Armstrong's name appeared. Moments later Sylvester's showed up.

"Holy shit," Scott said when he saw their names.

A second list began. I recognized some of the names of former students. "These names are by types they would service. Here's the males for males." I pressed the advance arrow. "The males for females." I pressed it again. "And females for males." I saw Greg's sister's name. I pressed the button once more. The last list had females for females.

"Armstrong and Sylvester were customers of Sheila's," I guessed. "That's why she called."

"That's got to be it," Scott said.

I examined the second list. Next to the names were physical characteristics: age, weight, height, color of hair and eyes. None was over twenty-five, one as young as fourteen. Evans was a pimp, and not a cheap one. He kept a large percentage of each whore's take to keep them from making enough money to get big ideas. The costs were next to the names. The lowest was $100 for an hour. The fourteen-year-old was a girl for $5,000 a night. I felt sick.

Scott said, "Evans was a fucking creep."

"Yeah," I agreed.

"You know this is dangerous information," Scott said.

"You're right. Whoever is in charge of Adonis-at-Large must know Evans had this information. They must want it back."

"Maybe Evans was in charge."

"Maybe, but I don't think that was his style. He leached from others. Certainly an operation this big has others involved. Maybe this is what they broke into the Evanses' house looking for."

I pressed the arrow to run the information again. I hoped it would give some clue we'd missed as to who was in this with Evans. But checking the whole entry gave no hint of whom this might be. Whoever it was, I also suspected it was the one Evans owed money to.

"If there is somebody else, maybe Neil would know," Scott suggested.

"I'll try him later." I looked at the end of the program thoughtfully. I had a grim thought. "You know what else bothers me," I said.

"What?" he asked.

"Daphne's comment made me think of this. Remember when she said 'where all pretty young men go.' And that's how Neil described Adonis-at-Large the other day, lots of pretty young men."

"If Evans was part of the operation he peddled his own kid. Nobody could be that vile," Scott said. "And wait, Phil didn't say anything like that."

"Maybe he didn't know his dad was behind it." I ran the information back searching for Phil's name. It wasn't there.

"So he wasn't part of the group," Scott concluded.

I shrugged. "Maybe not or maybe Phil just became part of the group since he left home."

The last set of information on Sylvester and Armstrong revealed the connection among the three of them. They had been skimming money from athletic events, as Meg had suggested. The how and why I wasn't sure yet. I was determined to find out at school that day. I told Scott my plan.

"Shouldn't you take all this to the police?" he objected.

"You forget, they have a copy."

"You know what I mean."

"Okay. They probably haven't broken into the program yet." We were in the bedroom. I talked while I undressed for a quick shower. "I'll tell you what I'll do. After we've talked to Mrs. Evans after school, we'll go straight to the police station."

He looked dissatisfied.

I went on quickly. "Before I leave I'll make another copy of the disc. Plus I want to run copies on the printer. I'll need one for school." I jumped into the shower. "We can mail one copy to your place and one here. That way the information will be in many places, and available to us if someone decides to get nasty."

"They've already gotten nasty," he pointed out.

"You were there to rescue me." I opened the shower curtain and grinned at him.

"Barely," he grumbled, "and I still think we should tell the police now."

"After school, I promise."

Scott wrote Keith a note in case he woke up while we were gone.

We left with one disc and two printouts. I left one disc at home for Scott to examine during the day. We mailed the printouts on the way to school. Scott looked worried all the while he drove.

I gave his hand a reassuring pat. "Everything will be all right. I wouldn't miss this day at school for the world. I can't wait to meet with Armstrong and Sylvester. It's time to push the bullies around a little."

"I wish this was over with and we were out of it," he said.

"We didn't ask to be in it," I replied.

"What about Phil?" he asked.

"I don't know. I'm worried, but I can't think of what we could do."

"We could try Greg's sister."

"We didn't get too far with her before, but I'm willing to give it another try. She should be able to give us a lead on the escort service."

Scott planned to pick me up at school after staying with Keith all day. Together the three of us would go see Mrs. Evans. I was to call Scott immediately if there was a problem with the administrators. As I got out he told me to be careful. I promised I would.

The first thing I did was go to the school office. I asked Georgette to tell Armstrong and Sylvester I wanted to see them in my classroom at noon.

"Tell them?" She gasped faintly.

"Yes, Georgette."

She gaped at me. "What if they're busy?"

"Tell them they need to cancel it, or they can cancel their careers."

If they were sufficiently angry and off balance when they showed up I might be able to get solid information out of them.

Between classes I borrowed a computer from Meg. I filled her in briefly on the latest and told her I'd give her the details later.

All morning I half expected one or the other of them to come down or send a message refusing the meeting. It's seldom that job-threatening conversations occur in the school system, and even rarer for the teacher to be the one doing the threatening. For a fleeting moment I let myself enjoy the irony of the situation. Around eleven I found myself a little tired. I shook it off. I hoped to be through with the Evans family, the administration, and the murder by the end of the day.

At noon they showed up.

Sylvester's shallow face now had red blotches I'd never seen before. He rubbed his hands together in nervous bursts.

Armstrong gave me a look that combined condescension with benign puzzlement. He said, "If you wanted to see us, it wasn't necessary to terrorize a poor, lowly secretary. A simple request would have been quite sufficient." He attempted what I supposed he thought was a wise-fatherly smile. To me it looked vinegary and pained.

I said, "Gentlemen, I have some information for you. It should clarify a lot of the problems we've had around here."

"I have a meeting in ten minutes," Armstrong said, "so if you could be quick about it."

I flipped the computer on. I invited them to join me in viewing the screen.

"Oh, no." Sylvester moaned as he realized what it was. He sat down heavily into one of the student's desks, covering his face with his hands.

Armstrong decided to brave it out. "I can't imagine what you think this jumble of dates and dollar amounts means," he said to me. "Obviously this is something Jim Evans dreamed up. You can't imagine we have anything to do with the random actions of a man who isn't here to explain whatever it is you think you have here."

"I never mentioned Jim Evans," I said.

Sylvester's moan increased in depth and despair.

"Shut up," Armstrong barked at him. He turned to me.

"This is obviously some trick of yours to ruin us or get back at us. It won't work. We know you're gay. If this information comes out about us, we'll tell the world about you." All of his suave condescension was gone.

I kept my voice deadly calm. "That didn't work Tuesday. It won't work today. I'm still not impressed by your threats. You should know that the police have this data disc with this information on it."

"Then why haven't they talked to us?" Armstrong asked quickly.

"I figured out the access code only this morning. I haven't given it to the police yet, but I intend to."

"What can we do to stop you?" Sylvester asked.

"You're a cheap blackmailer like Evans," Armstrong accused.

"No," I said. "I'm trying to solve the murder. I want you to tell me the whole story. What hold did Evans have over you two?" I knew Scott would be angry at my next promise, but I felt it was necessary. "If you tell me, I won't give the police the access code."

"Forget it," Armstrong snapped. "You're not to be trusted."

"It was all so simple at first," Sylvester began.

"Shut your stupid mouth," Armstrong roared at him.

"That's all I've been these years, your stupid dupe. Can't you see it's all going to come out? I'll lose my job"—Sylvester pointed at Armstrong—"and so will you."

"It won't come out if we stick together." Armstrong pointed at me. "What can he do? He's only a schoolteacher."

But Sylvester was a broken man. His body sagged and drooped around the student desk. He tried to reason with Armstrong. "The police will find out about all this. We're going to be implicated in the murder. If we talk now it might go easier for us."

"We haven't done anything," Armstrong insisted.

Sylvester turned to me, "I know I had nothing to do with the murder, absolutely nothing. I want that clear."

"Meaning I did?" Armstrong said.

"I don't know. Did you?" Sylvester responded.

"You son of a bitch." Armstrong swung his arm to hit his employee. Sylvester didn't flinch. I seized the arm on the back swing.

Armstrong turned to me, "You think you're so high and mighty," he began.

Sylvester cut him off. "Jason, it's time to drop it." His voice was weary.

Armstrong leaned over Sylvester, "The police already have a suspect." He flapped his arm in my direction. "They won't listen to him. Don't say anything stupid."

Sylvester waved his boss away and looked up at me.

While Sylvester explained Armstrong strode to the window and contemplated the world outside.

Sylvester said, "Six years ago I needed money. I was getting divorced. I'd gotten my mortgage when interest rates were out of sight. There were other things too. It doesn't matter what. I was desperate. It all seemed so simple. For years they'd trusted me with counting the receipts from all school events. It was a practice left over from fifteen or twenty years ago when this was a little farm district and one man ran the whole operation."

He sighed heavily. "So I started skimming money. At first it was small amounts—a hundred a week from the football games. It turned out it was incredibly easy. During basketball season there was a lot more money. No one kept count of how many people showed up at the games. It was a poor month when I didn't get an extra thousand.

"Then I got caught." He jerked his thumb at Armstrong. "I don't know how he did it. I was so careful not to let the numbers fluctuate too much. The basketball team won all its home games that year. Crowds were enormous. He came to my office late one night after a basketball game. Maybe he was suspicious before then. I don't know. I'm certain he never intended to turn me in. Instead he had one of his oily proposals. I had to go along." He gave me a look that appealed for sympathy.

I sat on the edge of my desk prepared to listen to the rest. He went on. "I was to continue skimming money. He would take half. I had to go on taking risks. The next year I was in better financial shape, and I wanted to stop. He told me we would keep on. That if I tried to stop he'd turn me in. I said he'd be fired too. He laughed at me and dared me to quit. I couldn't chance it. I needed the job."

Sylvester snuffled. He fished for a handkerchief, found none. He wiped his nose and face on his coat sleeve. "He's a greedy bastard. That's what wrecked it. We kept on and Evans found out about it."

"How?" I asked.

"Some stupid assignment he gave the kids in math class. It was a group of slow kids. He told them to count how many kids fit in each bleacher section of the gym—some stupid thing like that. One of the god-damn kids got hold of one of those counter things. He sat at the door counting every kid who walked in the gym. This way he wouldn't have to count the kids in each section. He could simply divide the total by the number of sections, and that's easier than trying to count each section with all the kids constantly moving around."

Futilely he fished for a handkerchief again. Before he abused his sleeve once more, I handed him a tissue from the box on my desk.

I gave him a minute then prodded, "So the kid got an accurate count."

"Yes. Later, Evans told us he was the only kid who completed the assignment along with extra credit, which was to multiply the number of kids by the price of admission. Evans remembered the assignment. It was the only one the kid turned in all year. Evans remembered the totals too. Besides being a math teacher, Evans had an incredible memory for statistics.

"When the student paper, as it always does, printed the amount of the gate receipts, Evans noticed the discrepancy. For several games he sat with a counter. When the disparity happened consistently he figured illegal activity was in progress.

"He came to me with it. I refused to face him alone. I brought him to Armstrong. We worked out a deal. Evans would get a percentage. For five years I've paid the price. My health is shot. My stomach is in shreds. And I'm the one who counts the money. I'm the one they'll blame."

Armstrong turned and faced us. "No one will do anything if you keep your mouth shut."

"I won't let them pin a murder charge on me."

"No one said anything about murder," Armstrong said.

"The police will," I countered. "They'll see blackmail as a good motive for murder."

He walked over to me, "And what makes you a big deal know-it-all?"

"Remember," I said, "I'm just a schoolteacher."

"I'll drag you down with us," Armstrong threatened.

"I'm not worried about me. I know I didn't kill him."

Armstrong glared at me.

I turned to Sylvester and asked, "Where were you the night of the murder?"

"Home with my wife," he said simply. He'd remarried three years ago.

I turned back to the superintendent. "And where were you, Mr. Armstrong?"

"I don't have to answer your god-damn questions." He gave me an evil stare. I gazed calmly back. Finally his eyes dropped.

Sylvester said, "You might as well know the rest. We were in the gambling operation too." He waved a hand in Armstrong's direction. "He met with Evans that night to pay everything."

"You god-damned son of a bitch." This time I wasn't quick enough to stop him. Armstrong belted Sylvester in the mouth with the back of his hand.

Sylvester's head rocked back. His nose began to bleed. Armstrong swung around to me. He snarled, "Yes, I met Evans to pay what we owed him."

"What time was this?"

"About twelve-thirty."

"Why then?"

"That's when he said to meet him. I think he enjoyed making things inconvenient and uncomfortable for people."

"You paid what you owed?"

"And I left. I swear he was alive and sitting in the restaurant parking lot when I left him."

"How did your gambling get started?" I asked.

"He insisted we join his gambling operation. He made it part of the price we had to pay for his silence."

"Did you know any of the details of the operation?"

"No, not really," Armstrong said, "only that he handled everything."

"Tell the rest of it," Sylvester said, "about that night."

Armstrong gave him a dirty look. "All right. Along with paying him I told him we wouldn't gamble any more. These past two months we lost more money from the gambling than we took in from skimming off money."

"What'd he say to your refusal to pay?"

"He said he'd expose us if we failed to come across as usual the next week. He died before we found out if it was a bluff or not."

"I didn't kill him," Sylvester reiterated. "I was at home."

"Did you kill him?" I asked Armstrong.

He sat on top of the desk next to Sylvester. He gazed up at me. "I don't expect you to believe me, but no, I didn't kill him. I might have during that week some time. Some lucky guy got there ahead of me."

I dropped my next question innocently into the conversation. "And you were customers of the escort service?"

"Only once, only once," Sylvester said. "She was over eighteen. I made sure of that."

"After the fact." Armstrong sneered.

"I didn't even know it was a former student until afterward," Sylvester said. "You had sex with her too," he added.

"That's why she called you," I said.

"Once you were caught in Evans's web it only got worse," Armstrong said.

During the day I made another decision. After school I spoke to Greg. I talked to him about going to see his sister with us. He agreed to come along. I hoped his presence would convince her to tell us more. We'd pick him up later.

I called Murphy. He didn't think they'd reopen the case, but he would keep trying. I wanted to tell about Armstrong's meeting with Evans, but I'd promised them. Slime as they were, I wouldn't break my promise to them—at least for now. If I couldn't prove Vance didn't do it in a day or so I'd have to. I asked Murphy if I could talk to Vance. He said he'd try to arrange it.

When I got in the car Keith moved to the backseat.

"I slept until one-thirty," Keith announced.

"I'm envious," I told him.

He picked up the stereo earphones in the backseat. "Do these work?" he asked. Scott adjusted the system for backseat headset listening. Scott's car stereo system is better than most people's home systems.

As Scott drove I filled him in on the big confrontation. I spoke low to be sure Keith couldn't hear even with his earphones on. I was annoyed at Scott's initial reaction.

He said, "So you won't give the police the access code?"

"I promised them if they told me I wouldn't."

"What about your promise to me?"

"I'm sorry. I wanted their information."

"And what about the other stuff on the disc? What about all those kids being used as prostitutes?" he demanded. "Are you going to tell about that?"

"Yes, I'm going to tell about that."

"Fine. When?" He was angry.

"Soon."

"Each minute you delay another kid is hurt, probably scarred for life."

"Will you ease off? I didn't apply for the position of God here. We were lucky we found the key to the whole operation. The police have the data. They haven't helped us. I'm not ready to help them."

"Think of the kids." He was still angry.

"Those on that list have been doing prostitution for a long time. Even with our immediate intervention there's little we could do."

"We could stop it."

"How?"

"If we told the cops."

"And they'd do what?"

"Arrest the kids."

"Yeah, so?"

"And it would stop."

"For how long?"

This held him silent for a minute. "They could return them to their parents," he said finally.

"These kids, or most of them, don't want to be with their parents. Long ago they could have returned to them. They didn't." I pointed my finger at him. "Or their parents don't want them. I agree we need to tell the police. My view is that it isn't as immediate an issue as you think it is."

"Say I agree to that. When you decide to give the information to the police, how will you keep from giving them the stuff about Armstrong and his buddy?"

"I don't know."

"Are you sure you've got a hold of yourself on this?"

"Yes," I said flatly. "I want to find the murderer. The police can't or won't. I found the body. I've been shot at and beaten up. I won't give in. Tell me if I'm wrong in how I'm handling this. If you want, turn the car around right now. We'll go straight to the police station."

Without a word he pulled the car to the side of the road. He jammed the gearshift into neutral.

"You can't park here," I said, staring straight ahead.

"Look at me," he commanded.

I did. His eyes searched mine, troubled and concerned. Very softly he said, "When you get stubborn you take yourself far away."

"I'm not being—"

He cut off my denial. "Yes, you are. You've got one thing in your head, finding the murderer, but you're making decisions you can't have as much confidence in as you pretend."

I opened my mouth to retort, but he said, "Let me finish, please."

Several drivers beeped their horns as they pulled around us. The shoulder was narrow, and we were only half off the road. I glanced back at Keith. He listened on the earphones contentedly.

The quiet thrum of Scott's angry voice filled the car. "Look, Tom, I don't disagree with what you've done. You're angry. So am I. You want to find the killer. So do I. We both want to protect those kids. Fine. I disagree with the order you have for solving this. I disagree with your protecting Sylvester and Armstrong. Your reasons are probably right. And I know you promised them. All of that's fine. But I've got a right to state my objections without you becoming so God-awful stubborn. That is not okay. That kind of stubbornness shuts me out. I don't like it when you distance yourself from me like that."

I listened to him. I watched his serious blue eyes. I saw the concern there. He'd called me on my stubbornness before. He was right. I got hold of my pride. I eased a couple of deep breaths in and out to give myself time to cool down. "I'm sorry, Scott. You're right. I got carried away." I gazed at him evenly.

He smiled gently. "Okay. We'll be all right." We resumed our trip to the Evanses' home.

After repeated knocking Mrs. Evans answered the door. Hair uncombed and makeup awry, she led us to the living room. Keith, still tired from last night's adventure, wandered upstairs without argument.

"I'm sorry Keith has been such trouble," she said softly and lifelessly.

"He's been no trouble," Scott said.

She folded her hands in her lap and stared at them. She looked lost and defeated.

I questioned her about her activities the night before.

She didn't answer my questions. Instead she plucked dispiritedly at the sleeve of her dress. She said, "My husband is dead. My oldest boy is gone. My family is lost." She continued speaking without expression or gesture. "I'm a rotten mother."

"Mrs. Evans," I said, "you've been under an awful strain. We realize that. We want to help."

"Yes, help," she echoed plaintively.

I tried again. "Mrs. Evans, what made you go hunting for Phil last night?" To her continued silence I said, "How did you know to go looking in that bar?"

"Everybody thought I didn't know anything. Half the time they treated me like I didn't exist."

"Who, Mrs. Evans?"

"Everyone. My husband, Phil, even Keith nowadays. But I listened to everything I could. I heard things."

I was afraid to press her, but I wanted any information she had.

"How did you hear?" I asked.

"Oh, on the phone, on the extension."

I was confused. "You did this last night?"

"No, when my husband was alive. When Phil was here."

"What did you find out when you listened?"

"Everything. I knew my husband was an evil criminal, all of it."

"All the illegal stuff?" Scott was incredulous.

"All."

"The prostitution? The gambling?" he continued.

"All is all," she said simply.

Now he was mad. "How could you keep silent?" he demanded.

She shrugged. "You weren't here. You didn't know what it was like. There was nothing that could be done."

I said, "Mrs. Evans, you claim to have secretly known what your husband was up to. In effect you snuck around gathering knowledge to no effective purpose."

"Yes," she whispered.

"Why didn't you tell all this to the police?" I asked.

Her voice became even softer. "I couldn't."

I shook my head. "Listen, Mrs. Evans, now you expect us to believe that somehow last night this magic knowledge led you to one particular gay bar?"

"That's part of it," she answered.

"And what's the other part? What made you go looking last night?"

"There was a call."

"From whom?"

"He didn't say."

I gritted my teeth. "What did he say?"

"'If you want to see Phil, you better come quick.'"

"And then he told you where to go?"

"Yes."

"What time was the call?"

"Around ten-thirty."

"You went by yourself?"

"Yes."

"Going to one bar doesn't take all night."

"I didn't find him there so I searched."

"Where?"

"I found one of those little magazines in that first bar that gives the addresses of gay places. I went up and down the streets."

"Clark, Halsted, Broadway?"

"All those, yes, and more."

"You went in all those gay bars?"

"Every one that was open. Every one that would let me in."

"All night you did this?"

"Yes."

"Why didn't you ask for help?"

"From who?"

"You asked me once."

"And you didn't bring Phil back."

"You withheld a great deal of information that could have helped me the first time you asked. Mrs. Evans, you don't make sense to me."

She responded in her softest tones yet. "The whole world doesn't make sense to me."

We sat and listened to time pass.

She didn't break down sobbing or go to pieces. She simply said, "It's all quite useless. Do as you wish. Take my children, my home, my life. I give up."

I wasn't about to leave her alone in this state. Before we left I called Heather Delacroix. Quickly I explained the situation to her. She promised to come over to handle the immediate problems of the Evans household. We waited for her to show up, then left.

We drove to Greg's house and picked him up. I introduced him to Scott. Scott's fifty-thousand-dollar sports car may have impressed him as much as meeting Scott. I explained everything to him about Phil's situation and the status of the Evans family. He seemed genuinely concerned about Phil's plight. I also told him about his sister and the disc. He didn't act too surprised about his sister's occupation. I asked him about this.

"She never told me," he said, "but I sort of guessed. Mostly I tried not to think about it. Who wants to admit his sister"—he paused—"does what she does?" he finished.

At first his sister wouldn't let us in. It was Greg's pleading that got us past the door. In the living room she sat more silent than a stone Buddha, but far less serene.

First Greg tried to get her to give us information about the escort service. She ignored him.

After several minutes of this I made my plea for help.

She didn't react to me. Instead she turned on Greg. "Why'd you come with them?" she said.

"I'm worried about Phil," he answered.

"Was he your lover?"

"No."

"Then what do you care?"

"He was my friend." Greg looked at us helplessly.

"Phil could be in a lot of danger," I said. "We need the name and address of whoever ran Adonis-at-Large with Jim Evans."

She snorted contemptuously at me.

"We know you worked for him, and you lied when you said you didn't know about the computer disc when we were here last. We found your name along with many others on the disc."

"Then why don't you go ask them?"

"They would be at least as reluctant as you, and far more surprised and threatened."

"That isn't my problem."

"Come on, Sheila," Greg pleaded, "be reasonable."

"I am being reasonable. I got my freedom and my live-lihood from Jim Evans and his service. I got out of the house. I've got my own place, a life of my own."

"But you're a whore," Greg said.

"That's right, little brother." Her answer was surprisingly mild.

"It's not right," Greg insisted.

"And what is?" she demanded quickly.

He opened his mouth to answer but none came. He flapped his arm on the chair in defeat.

I tried another tack. "You lied to us the first time we were here. You said you broke off with Evans three years ago."

"I didn't lie," she said. "I stopped screwing him three years ago. I never stopped working for him. You didn't ask the right questions."

"If I ask the right questions now will I get the truth?"

"I doubt it."

Her complacency infuriated me.

Greg said, "Sheila, I'm scared for Phil, and for you."

For the first time a slight softness crept into her voice. There was even a ghost of a smile on her lips. She said, "There's nothing to be frightened of, Greg."

"Then why won't you help?"

"It's my income, Greg. It's how I live."

From another room came the sounds of a waking baby. Sheila began to stand up, but Greg stopped her. "I'll get him," he said.

He returned with the child cradled confidently in his arms. He smiled at us shyly as he sat down next to his sister. "I baby-sit all the time." His teenage gawkiness had disappeared. Sheila smiled at the two of them. For a moment all the tension evaporated from the room.

Scott interrupted this domesticity. "Greg baby-sat while you went out to turn tricks?"

Greg looked crestfallen. Sheila swore. The phone rang.

She went into the kitchen to answer it. We couldn't hear the conversation. She was only on a minute and a half. We heard her hang up, but she didn't return for five minutes. When she came back she had changed from her old blue jeans and T-shirt top to a dress that clung so tight that the outline of her panties was clear underneath. She wore no bra. She had her winter jacket with her.

"Greg, could you sit tonight?" she asked.

"Sure," he said, dumbfounded. The baby was already asleep in his arms.

"Your friends are welcome to stay as long as you want them to."

"Sheila," I called to her retreating figure. But she slammed the door. We listened to her receding steps.

"I'm sorry," Greg said. "She's really a great person, honest."

I glanced rapidly around the living room. "Maybe there's some clue in the apartment," I said.

Greg began a protest, but I was up and moving. Scott followed. Burdened with the baby, Greg was too slow to stop us. How much opposition he'd have shown I don't know. His feelings seemed torn. I gave a brief word of assurance to him as I started to hunt.

We searched all the rooms. Besides the living room, there were only the kitchen, bedroom, and bathroom. Greg followed us watching from the doorways.

After thirty minutes we came up empty. We'd even found the dope hidden in a fake frozen orange juice can in the refrigerator freezer. Finally we stood in the bedroom looking at each other helplessly.

"I'm really sorry, you guys," Greg said. He still held the baby. I ran my eye back over the room. Green wallpaper hung on the wall. The floor was bare wood. The bed had no headboard. The blanket was thin and patched. The dresser showed signs of several poorly done refinishing jobs. The only bit of color was the baby's crib. I held up the tiny mattress of the crib, idly thunking it against the dresser. "It's hopeless," I said.

"Is that something?" Greg asked.

"Where?" I asked.

He pointed at the back of the mattress.

"That's the do-not-remove-under-penalty-of-whatever tag," Scott said.

"No, on the back of it," Greg said.

I'd only glanced at the label, now I looked more closely. Inked to the back of it was a list of names, addresses, and phone numbers.

"Clients," Scott guessed.

"Maybe, but look at these." I indicated the bottom two listings.

"What about them?" Scott asked.

"They're the only ones without a name and not in the Joliet area," I said.

"Maybe they're special clients," Scott said.

"Possibly, but look again at the addresses. This one with the line through it is the Evanses' address in Mokena, I'm almost certain. Now look at this address underneath it on Orleans Street in Chicago. It's in separate color ink."

Greg asked, "What does that mean?"

I examined the addresses again. I mulled over the possibilities for several minutes. Then I said, "I think it was added recently, probably since Evans's death. I bet it's her new contact. Now look at the address itself. That's this year's trendy section of the city, from the Merchandise Mart north to Chicago Avenue and east from the river to Lake Michigan. And I think this is the address of the art gallery of John North, an extremely wealthy gay artist, bar owner, and activist. He lives in this old gargantuan three-story house that's wedged between two highrises. I pointed the block out to you, Scott, the last time we came home from Carson's Ribs."

"I think I remember," Scott said.

"I'm sure of it. In the old house the art gallery is the first two floors. He lives above it."

I ripped off the label. Leaving Greg there, we drove to the city.

"We can't just barge in there," Scott said as we drove through the November night.

"Yes, we can," I said. "I think those two addresses are connected. My guess is Evans and North were in this together."

"That's a hell of a stretch of the imagination."

"It's all we've got."

His okay sounded fatalistic.

"What I want to know," I said, "is who called Mrs. Evans. And I also want to know what happened between that call and the one Keith received from Phil. There's over an hour gap that is unexplained. And I want to know why the person called."

"You don't want much," Scott said.

"If I can answer those questions, we'll be able to find Phil and I bet be a long way to finding the murderer."

"You think there's a connection?"

"Between the murder and the kid's disappearance?"

"Yeah."

"If you'd asked me that a couple days ago, I'd have said no. Now I'm almost certain there is. We'll find it."

Later as we drove onto the Ohio Street off ramp, Scott said, "I'm surprised at the number of lies you and I have been told."

"I'm not," I replied. "They all want to protect themselves. I think it's fairly normal."

For my money the Ohio Street off ramp at night offers the most beautiful view of Chicago's skyline. It led directly to the section of town we wanted. Even on a Thursday night there were lines of people trying to get into Ditka's, Ed Debevic's, and the Hard Rock Cafe. We had to park six blocks away and walk back.

A couple of quick hot dogs from a sidewalk vendor provided us with dinner.

We arrived at the house. Turrets and battlements jutted from odd corners. Bay windows and cupolas existed at strange angles. The thing had obviously been built in sections, none of which matched.

Cars swished toward the Ontario Street on ramp to the Kennedy Expressway as we examined the building.

A faint glow from a third-floor window was the only sign of life.

John North, the owner, was the most up-and-coming artist and photographer in town. Last January one of the papers declared him this year's Renaissance man. He was the cutting edge of trendiness.

He was gay. He occasionally deigned to appear at fundraisers for gay community events, staying long enough to captivate the prettiest boy there and then leaving. He was a strikingly handsome man in his late twenties. The world was at his feet. The dishier parts of my information came from Neil. He hated him. Despite repeated promises, North hadn't shown up at an important fund-raiser Neil had organized. Neil neither forgave nor forgot.

There was no downstairs bell to ring, only the closed glass doors through which we could see some of his latest constructions.

Banging on the doors brought no response. "This is useless. Let's try the back," I said.

The alley that led to the back was unlit, shadows upon shadows flowing back into deeper dimness as we walked further in. Garbage spilled and scrunched underfoot. We heard vermin and critters hurry away at our approach. An occasional pair of eyes glared insolently from a garbage heap before winking out.

A wooden gate gave entry to the backyard of the house. We slipped inside. I closed the gate. The latch clicked. The backyard was a jumble of six-foot evergreens and taller, more distant trees. Broken bits of sidewalk poked at our feet as we tiptoed down the narrow path to the back porch. The chill November wind whistled above us, crackling the barren tree branches together. In the closeness of the backyard, sheltered by the evergreens, I could feel only the faintest traces of a breeze on my cheek. Total darkness emanated from the rear of the house. A porch ran the length of the back of the house.

I put a foot on the bottom step. Scott put a hand on my sleeve to stop me.

"We're going to get caught." His voice was low.

"No, we aren't." I, too, kept my voice down.

"I'm glad you're confident. What if someone catches us?"

"I thought six-foot-four baseball heroes didn't get scared."

"I'm not scared," he whispered fiercely, "I'm worried, that's all."

"Don't be." Where I got these calm assurances I don't know. My armpits overflowed with sweat.

We ascended the creaking and crumbling stairs. We stopped at the vague outline of the back door.

"Do we knock?" Scott whispered sarcastically.

"Why are we whispering?" I whispered.

"It's spooky back here, and we don't belong, that's why." Scott spoke next to my ear or I wouldn't have heard him.

"We knocked, or rather banged, at the front door," I said in an almost normal voice. "We'll simply knock." I raised my arm to do so.

A laughing and singing group turned into the alley.

I stood absolutely still.

"What if they're coming here?" Scott's whisper was angry.

As they drew closer several of the voices became distinct. Their obvious drunken state did not comfort me.

Their movement down the alley proceeded at a glacial pace. They stood outside the gate for an eternity. I held my breath.

The gate clicked open.

Scott grabbed me, prepared, I suppose, to sprint bullishly through them. Instead I wrenched him back into the deeper darkness of the porch corner farthest from the alley. I almost pulled him too hard. We nearly toppled off the edge.

The group walked swiftly now. They ascended the porch. The darkness, their good spirits, and their general state of inebriation kept us hidden. I listened to one of them fumble with a key in the lock. The door opened. A moment later a light sprang on in the house. I could see there were five of them. Bundled up as they were, I didn't recognize any of them.

"When are the rest going to get here?" the last one in asked as he entered.

"Couple minutes" came a deep voiced reply from inside the house. "They went to park their cars."

The door creaked shut. I found myself breathing for the first time in a forever.

"Let's get the hell out of here," Scott rasped.

"No, I want to see what's going on. If there are a lot of people showing up, we could simply join the throng."

"You're nuts. These people know each other."

I shushed him. I looked through a gap in the curtains in the window next to us. It was an entry room. After hanging up coats and scarves, the five of them quickly passed through a farther door and out of sight. They left the light on.

The gate clicked open again. Another group of five or six walked in. I could see them more clearly from the lights the first group had left on.

In a rush it dawned on me that they would be able to see us too. Scott gave a low moan. I assumed he had the same thought.

"What luck finding a parking space so close," one of them said.

I threw my arms around Scott and locked him in a fierce embrace. He started to protest, but I covered his mouth with my lips. His stifled mumble ended as he realized my plan.

Heavy footsteps ascended the porch.

"Look at those two." Someone tittered.

"How decadent," another added.

The door creaked open. They stomped into the house.

The last man stuck his head back out the door. "You guys will freeze your asses off out there. Better come in before the rest of the crowd gets here if you want to be up close."

"Thanks," I mumbled. Whoever it was went in.

Scott broke the embrace. "Let's leave."

"Let's go in."

"You're crazy."

"We were invited."

"He thought we were one of them."

"There'll probably be a crowd. He said so. We can get lost among them." I tried to give my words a confidence and reasonableness I'm not sure I felt.

"We've seen ten maybe eleven guys at most," Scott said.

"Phil could be in some kind of danger in there."

"Fine, call the police."

"After all this your continued faith in the regular constabulary continues to amaze me. Remember, they don't want to reopen the case."

We heard another group coming down the alley.

"We'll look just as suspicious walking out past them."

"No, we won't," Scott said.

"I'm not going to stand here arguing. I'm going in." I walked to the door and reached for the knob. I looked back at Scott.

The gate clicked open again. Another group entered the yard.

"All right," Scott grumbled.

The back of the house was a warren of storage rooms connected by a twisting hallway. There was a narrow uncarpeted stairway leading up. The thumping from a thunderous stereo system beckoned us upward. The people we'd heard behind us caught up. They greeted us in a friendly manner, and made no remarks about us being unfamiliar, unexpected, or unwelcome. We let them pass and followed them upstairs.

As we entered the third floor the thudding of the stereo eased into an ethereal blues song, much easier on the ears. Eventually we discovered that the third floor consisted of two huge rooms. The back half, in which we stood as we entered, was essentially a kitchen–living-room area. The track lighting that snaked around the ceiling was turned quite low. The dimness deemphasized the jungle of gay gothic decor.

A new group had come in behind us. After depositing our coats in a pile on a couch in this room, we followed the crowd into the second room.

Here the ceiling and floor were flat black. Mirrors completely covered the walls. The only opening in the room was the door through which we entered. A bed, ten feet by ten feet, covered with a black leather spread, sat in the middle of the floor. The lighting came from soft white glows concealed in the floor in the four corners.

More than thirty men milled about the room, others rapidly entering. No one took particular notice of us. We drifted to a corner attempting to look at ease and as if we belonged.

The other furniture consisted of what you would find in any well-equipped dungeon—a torture rack, shackles and chains, a contraption that somewhat resembled a child's swing, and a table filled with a variety of whips.

The men formed a tight circle around the swing. One of them I thought to be John North. He was dressed in a conservative gray business suit, as were half the others in the room. Some wore jeans and casual shirts. A few were in full leather drag.

"I don't think I'm going to like this," Scott whispered.

"Predicting the future is a risky business," I whispered back.

From out of the center of the group a naked male climbed aboard the swing. The men around him murmured approval. I stifled a gasp. For a second I thought it was Phil, but the swing twirled and I saw the face clearly. It was a stranger. Although he had about the same build as Phil, he was considerably younger. If this kid was over fifteen, I was over ninety. He spread his legs and then reached over his head to grip the chains above. They shackled him by wrist and ankle to the swing.

"We have to put a stop to this," I whispered.

At that moment one of the guests walked up to us. A dozen cows may have died attempting to make him butch. It hadn't worked. His lisp and limp wrist showed through the leather. Thick greasy hair reached to his shoulders. He might have been around thirty. He had a pronounced beer gut, the source of which became evident when he breathed on us.

"Don't I know you?" he said to Scott.

"I don't think so," Scott demurred.

"Well, I think I do," the man stated, assuming the belligerence of a drunkard. In a minute he would get loud and draw attention to us.

He jabbed a finger into Scott's chest. "Anybody as pretty as you I'd never forget. I think you're some movie star." His voice began to rise. One or two of the other guests glanced in our direction.

With an aplomb that surprised me I heard Scott say, "Maybe you saw me on the cover of one of the national sports magazines."

"You mean one of those terribly virile magazines for the sweat-drenched set?"

"Sort of," Scott said.

"Oooh," he crooned. He smiled and put his hand on Scott's hip. "And why did they put you on the cover?"

"I pitched two no-hitters in the World Series."

"Oooh, how wonderful. Is that world thing football or baseball"—he scratched his head—"or hockey?"

Further explanation became unnecessary when one of the drunk's buddies came over and took his arm. Let's go, Edgar," he said, "it's time to start." He led Edgar away.

"That was fairly cool and collected," I said.

"I practice a lot with reporters," he replied.

All eyes were on the swing. Edgar picked up one of the whips. Deep, expectant voices murmured around us.

Obviously we couldn't grab the kid and run. Even if we could get to him, we'd have to unlock his shackles while fending off the mob. If we in some way could yank the boy down undamaged, there were fifty of them and only two of us. Most of them were far more burly, and probably more dangerous, than Edgar. I doubted we'd get information from North tonight anyway. Coming back during business hours tomorrow seemed a reasonably sane alternative.

I wanted to leave right then, but I couldn't. Not with a thirteen- or fourteen-year-old ready to be a plaything for what I presumed was tonight's orgy.

The one door to the room swung open again. Daphne marched in.

"Oh, shit," I muttered.

"Let's break for it," Scott urged.

I put a restraining hand on his arm. "Easy, casual. Let's slip over toward the door. They'll be concentrating on center stage." We inched our way around the walls. I figured we could ease out, get downstairs, and make Scott's dream come true—call the cops.

We started in the far corner of the room from the door. An inch at a time, as casually as possible, we made our way around the fringes of the crowd. We were halfway when I saw Daphne begin to turn her bulk in our direction. I swiveled around hoping to cover us both. I waited breathlessly.

Scott peered around my ear carefully. He nodded, jerked his head a quarter inch toward the door. I turned around again. Daphne, her face turned away from us, chatted amiably with one of the guests.

Five minutes later we were three-quarters of the way to the door. Then with only a few feet to go a voice shouted, "Hold it, you two." I recognized Daphne's commanding bellow. "Grab them," she yelled.

We bolted for the door. Too late. They grabbed us from all sides. We struggled mightily. Scott went down a moment before me, snowed over by the crush of strong arms and bodies.

"Take them downstairs and keep them secure," Daphne ordered.

I saw John North peer over her shoulder. "Who are they?" he asked.

"Creeps and fools," she hissed. "Get them out of here," she commanded.

Roughly and unceremoniously they shackled us and dragged-carried us downstairs. As they escorted us out of the room I heard one voice, I thought it was Edgar's, suggest they use us for the next show on the swing. They secured us to a couple of kitchen chairs in a storeroom on the first floor.

They left us in the dark. In the dimness from the strip of light at the bottom of the door I could see Scott.

"Are you all right?" Scott asked.

"Maybe a couple bruises. You?"

"I'm fine."

Scott asked, "Now what, Sherlock?" I appreciated the lack of sarcasm in his voice.

"In the stories, Sherlock Holmes never got caught and tied up," I answered.

"Worse luck for us." He paused, then continued. "If these people killed Evans they may decide to get rid of us too."

"I know. I'm sorry I got you into this."

"I'm glad you did." His smile flashed in the dimness.

"You are?"

"Yeah, why not? I warned you a million times, but I went along. It's like an adventure."

"Thanks. I hope there's a happy ending."

"Me too," he said.

While trying to get loose we discussed options and possibilities. We got nowhere with either activity.

When finally the door opened it was John North himself who entered. He turned on a light and shut the door. His first action surprised me. He unshackled us. I rubbed life back into my wrists. When I looked at my watch I saw we'd been in the room two hours.

North leaned his back against the door. He was tall, blond, and blue eyed. His suit, impeccably cut, hung on him perfectly.

He folded his arms over his chest. "Well, gentlemen." His voice was well modulated, pleasing, and smooth. "What can I do for you?" I heard neither sarcasm nor humor in his tone. He might have been a polite clerk in an expensive boutique trained exclusively to be helpful.

"Daphne told you everything," I said.

"I have Daphne's version, yes. Now I'd like to hear yours." I told him. He listened attentively.

"And so," I summed up, "I think you know where Phil is. I think you have information that could tell who the killer is."

Scott spoke for the first time. "We know you're fucking slime from what we saw upstairs."

North raised an elegant eyebrow at Scott. He smiled slightly and chose to begin his explanations with Scott's remark.

"Did that bother you?" North asked him.

"Very much."

"And why?"

"It was a kid."

North chuckled. "But nothing else about it?"

"Adults can play whatever sexual games they want so far as I'm concerned," Scott said.

"And you don't think kids play sexual games?" he asked.

"Not that kind," I said.

But North was partly right. I know people don't like to admit it, but many kids are sexually active. The vast majority of parents prefer to think of their children as living lives of pristine innocence—and this is true for many. But as a schoolteacher helping troubled kids, I'd heard many stories about them and sex. One sophomore claimed that in sixth grade he kissed all but one of his female classmates and had been to bed with four of them. This didn't count the seventh- and eighth-grade girls who'd pursued him to orgasm. I found out he wasn't lying a year later from a girl who'd been part of his harem. For the kids the time between after school and when their parents came home from work gave a new meaning to play time.

"What you're doing up there isn't right," Scott said.

North gave him a condescending smile. "I suppose you're right," he said offhandedly. He moved away from the door.

I saw Scott ready to leap for the exit. North saw it too. He said, "There's no need for violent heroics. You gentlemen are free to go anytime. I'd prefer to explain, and I'm sure you have more questions."

Scott gave him a suspicious look.

North said to him, "Your little victim upstairs is long gone."

He began pacing the room slowly, hands in his pants pockets. He said, "So, you consider me a completely evil person?"

"God-damn right," Scott said.

"Now, let's consider what I've done. I've taken the child upstairs off the streets. He is drug free and has a warm place to sleep. His parents have been contacted and assured he is safe. They didn't care. Neither the mother nor the stepfather wanted him around. Six months ago the boy indiscriminately sold himself, living in doorways and alleys. He had syphilis and gonorrhea. I had him cleaned up and kept him that way. At that time I had him take the AIDS antibodies test. By some miracle he came out negative. I had him tested again two weeks ago. He was still negative. Now he only does safe sex."

He stopped in front of us, hands extended, almost begging for understanding. "Tell me," he challenged, "what is wrong with that picture?"

"That was one kid," I said. "There are other kids we saw on the computer."

"I've helped every one of them, most not as extensively as my example, but some nearly so, and all of them to some extent. At the very least they are all drug free, disease free, and trained to do only safe sex. People want prostitutes and kinky sex no matter what the danger. I give it to them safely."

"It's still wrong," Scott muttered.

North looked at me. I said nothing. He sighed deeply and went back to leaning against the door.

Maybe he and Daphne considered themselves worthy of good citizenship medals. I didn't. I hadn't changed my mind about him, but then again, I wasn't quite as prepared to condemn him as I had been.

"You have other questions?" he said. He quickly began answering, anticipating the obvious. "Your main question, of course, is did I kill Evans? No, I didn't. Do I have an alibi for the night of the murder? One that is sufficient for the police, I'm sure. Beyond that"—he paused—"I should add that I also don't know who did kill him."

"Tell me about your relationship with Evans," I said.

"We were partners. Generally I supplied the customers while he supplied the workers. We never quarreled up to and including the murder. Our basic values merged wonderfully. We both loved money. I invested mine in my work. I have the impression he gambled his away, although we never discussed his personal finances."

I explained to him what I knew about the gambling operation.

"Doesn't surprise me," he commented. "Besides the reputed gambling, he always had a tiresomely new money-making scheme cooked up. He kept trying to tell me about them. I wouldn't listen."

"Why didn't you join in any of his schemes?"

"I have a great thing going here. I didn't need the pipe dreams of some heterosexual misfit from the suburbs."

"And you don't have dreams?"

"Mine are coming true, or don't you read the papers?"

"Your dreams might be about to come down on your head, once the police get the information we have," Scott said.

"Will it? If crime didn't pay, I'd agree with you. But it does pay, and extremely well. More important, my lawyers have been on top of this situation, especially since the murder. If I am mildly inconvenienced, I'd be surprised. Business may suffer for a short while, but it'll come back. People are always willing to pay for sex, and I'm willing to sell."

"You're that confident you're safe?" I asked. "You know the police have Evans's computer disc."

He laughed, "Ah, yes, the magic disc gave us quite a worry for a short time."

"I don't get it," I said.

"I suppose you do deserve an explanation." He scratched an ear thoughtfully. "It all started the night Evans was murdered. Edgar, who is my right-hand man, met with him around two that morning out in those frightful suburbs. Edgar is my collector. Evans had only a few thousand dollars. He owed us a great deal more. We'd carried him for several weeks. This was not good. He made many promises and offered us a fantastic deal. I might have accepted, but he started making threats. He claimed he had a computer disc filled with information that would ruin me. Edgar knew how I'd react to that, but he was diplomatic.

"To Evans, Edgar said the threats weren't necessary, and he thought for sure I'd agree to several of his proposals.

"Edgar came back here to talk to me. Evans was supposed to show up soon afterward. He never did. The next day when I learned about the murder I became concerned about the disc and what might be on it."

"You sent someone to break into the Evanses' home," I said.

"Right. They broke into the house at noon, took all the discs, and came back here. The discs were all ordinary school programs. I had to be sure so I sent someone dressed as a custodian to look into his room at school."

"And when they didn't find anything in his classroom," I said, "they checked the scene of the murder."

"They had to," North said. "They couldn't be sure."

"That's when I walked in on them," I said.

"Yeah. Edgar fired to scare you. He had no orders to kill."

"So that's who it was," I said.

"None of the discs we found had anything incriminating on them. We had a copy of the one you found, only without the school information on it. Evans and I kept our data current. That information says nothing about me. I'm safe. Evans's threat was a cheap bluff."

"How'd you know about the one I have?" I asked.

"That was an unfortunate set of circumstances."

"I'd like to hear it," I said.

"Certainly. When Evans died we notified all our workers

of the new arrangement. Who'd collect their money, who'd give them referrals."

"The basics," Scott opined.

"Yes. Among them, of course, was Sheila Davis."

It began to dawn on me.

"You went to visit her that night. She reported that to us. I was out and didn't get the message until the next day. I called her back. She told me about the disc you mentioned to her. I didn't know if yours was simply a duplicate or the disc Evans said could ruin me. I couldn't take the chance. In the meantime I had been informed of your meeting with Phil. I was displeased about that, extremely so.

"Here you were, two people in your do-good mode, getting in my way. Plus you had a disc, maybe a fatal one. That night I sent two men to warn you off and get the disc. I wanted to send Edgar, but he was out of town. I sent two new men. They screwed it up."

"I got a beating," I said.

"And it didn't scare you away," North said.

"You bastard," Scott said.

"Business is hell," North responded. "You did scare *them* away. I waited until Edgar got back. I sent him out this evening. Around five today he broke into your house."

"What!"

"Not to worry, he's a pro. He reconnected your security system. He told me nothing was disturbed. He found the printout and a copy of the disc. I went over them quickly earlier, and more thoroughly before I came down to talk to you. It's only a copy, not new information. I have nothing to fear from Evans, or you for that matter."

"What if I said there was another disc?" I said.

"There isn't. You're too honest. You'd have said two discs earlier when you mentioned giving one to the police."

We fell silent. I was stumped.

Finally North said, "If that's all you gentlemen need tonight, I'd like to get to bed."

We got to our feet. I remembered Phil. I asked about him. For an instant North's calm slipped, but the cool façade quickly returned. "The boy was here up until a few nights ago," he said.

"Here as what? Another poor waif you rescued off the street?"

"Not quite."

"Did you know who he was?"

"Not at first." Still leaning against the door, he put his hands in his pants pockets, crossed his legs at the ankles, and told us the story. "I have major parties here about once a month. The talented and the rich attend, along with the prettiest boys on the street."

"Daphne is your source for pretty boys," I interjected.

"Quite often, yes."

"Where is Daphne? How'd you get her to keep her claws off us?"

"Daphne is marvelous in many ways. We go back many years together. She tends to overreact, especially if she thinks there is an emergency. It is quite easy for me to handle her. I own seventy-five percent of her bar. I've saved her from a number of tight spots. She owes me a great many favors. She does as she is told."

"Oh," I said.

"Phil came along to the latest party about a week ago now. He had virtues I prize." I didn't ask what those were. I wasn't sure I wanted to know.

North continued. "He stayed here for a while. As we discussed, he met with you. Then yesterday afternoon he decided to leave."

"Why?"

"You'll have to ask him that."

"Where did he go? Where is he now?"

"I don't know. I am generous to my boys, but if they decide to leave they cease to concern me. He left quite voluntarily."

"He must have said something."

"Not to me."

"To someone."

"Not that I know of."

I explained about the phone calls. North looked genuinely puzzled. "He was a kid. Maybe he panicked," North offered.

"Or maybe someone decided to kill him as they did his father," I said.

"Perhaps."

"And it worries me he hasn't tried or been able to call since then. Do your boys live here while you protect them?"

"No, and I see where you're headed. You may not talk to them."

"You forget we have their addresses from the computer."

"You forget I have a much stronger hold over them than you do. You must also consider that I am acting benignly tonight. I could choose to be much the opposite."

I ignored his threat. "Could we look through this place for him?"

He smiled wearily. "If you wish. You'll not find him. If you did happen upon one of the other boys, I guarantee he wouldn't talk."

"Accepting the fact that he's gone, can't you help us find him?" Scott asked.

"I could, but I won't."

"Why not?" I asked.

"It's not my problem any longer. If he'd stayed I'd have taken care of him. He's gone, so—too bad."

He opened the door for us, holding it politely as we preceded him out.

"Why did you tie us up and now let us go so easily?" I asked.

"I may be mildly inconvenienced because the police have that disc, but you're no threat to me. Daphne gets too excited. Upstairs it was better to be safe for the moment."

As we got our coats on the third floor a thought struck me. "Who called Mrs. Evans to come find her kid?" I asked.

North looked at me curiously. "Sorry. Once again I don't know. But in all the things you've told me that seems to be the most strange."

By the time we got out of there it was after two A.M. I was bushed. With all this running around we still hadn't found Phil, and we didn't know who the killer was. We walked back to the car.

"I think Phil's in that house." Scott's footsteps scraped tiredly as he spoke. "Probably hidden in some tiny corner that we wouldn't recognize in a year's searching."

"He may be," I replied wearily. "I feel terrible about Phil." As we waited for the light to change across from the Limelight I said, "I'm not ready to give up."

"I'm too tired to go back there and storm the place," Scott said. "We were lucky this time."

"I don't want to go back there right now."

"Good."

We reached the car. I said, "We haven't solved the murder or found the kid."

"That we haven't." He patted his pockets hunting for his keys.

"I want to go see Neil," I announced.

"Now? At this hour?" He found the keys and unlocked the car. We got in.

"Yes, now. He'll be among the queens holding court at the Melrose. They gather there every night when the bars begin to close."

"Why do we need to see him? And why now, for Christ's sake?"

The street outside was quiet as we sat in the car arguing. I said, "Because we've wasted too much time already. The kid called around this time last night, maybe a little earlier. It's been twenty-four hours."

"And whatever's been done to him happened twenty-four hours ago," Scott cut in.

"Probably, but we don't know that."

"I'm tired. You're tired. We can catch a few hours' sleep at my place. We'll be fresh in the morning."

"I have to work in the morning."

"Take the day off, or let's wait until after school."

"No," I said, "we let the boy go once. We're partly responsible for anything that happens to him."

He put the key in the ignition and said, "You still didn't answer me about why Neil."

"He's the one I got my basic information on North from. I'm hoping he'll know more."

"Tom, that's not a big possibility to go chasing at two in the morning."

"I know, Scott, but it's at least some hope. I promise it'll be the last stop tonight."

"You promise?"

"Yeah, I swear by my best pink chiffon outfit."

"You don't have a pink chiffon outfit."

"So, I swear by yours."

"I don't have one either."

"Scott, start the damn car. Melrose and Broadway."

"I know where it is."

Neil was there. Crammed into the corner booth were five of them all in their finest drag outfits. Neil spotted us and waved us over.

"You're here for high tea with the queens?" he asked.

"We need to see you, Neil."

My demeanor must have communicated the urgency and importance of my request. We moved to a back booth so we couldn't be overheard.

I told him what happened. His first reaction was "So, you've been in the sacred precincts. Half the queens in the city would kill for one of his invitations. Plus you made it all the way to the third floor. I am impressed. Gold stars for both of you." Then Neil launched into an anti-North tirade.

I stopped him. I said, "I agree, he's a despicable son of a bitch in designer clothing, but we need information, Neil. We've got to find the kid."

"If he's out there, I can't help you. He could be anywhere."

"What about North?" I asked. "Where does he send his rejects? The boys he's tired of—what happens to them?"

Neil hesitated, grumbled low, and looked away. I'd never seen him try to be evasive and distant before. "Nothing happens," he said. His hand shook as he raised his cup of tea for a sip. I'd never seen him lose his cool.

"Neil, you've got to tell us."

"I can't."

"The boy's life could depend on it," I said.

"It might," he admitted.

Scott and I pleaded and cajoled for fifteen minutes.

Neil still refused. He said, "John North has power in this city. In the gay community he knows all and sees all. He has queens begging to be his spies. Anyway, for what I've heard I have no proof, no certain knowledge, and I don't want it either. If it got out it could destroy me, a great deal of this community, and, of course, John North."

"Please." I explained again what we'd been through. What it meant to us. I added, "You want to see him taken down a few pegs, maybe hurt badly. This is your chance."

He glanced from Scott to me. All trace of theatrical effeminacy evaporated from his manner. Beneath the makeup I could see the frightened man.

He took out a hanky and wiped it across his upper lip. "All right," he said.

Neil looked over his shoulder to make sure no one was near, then leaned closer. He said, "This information is dangerous—not only for the reasons I said before—I mean for you personally. Be careful with it. These are only rumors, you understand. Of course, I believe them, but that's because I hate John North." He lowered his head and leaned further across the table. He whispered, "He makes porno movies, kiddie porn and worse. Many of his movies have sadomasochistic action." His words were so low that Scott and I were forced to bend almost half over to be close enough to hear. Our three heads were inches apart. "Some of the torture scenes are more than acting, and"—now his voice was lowest of all—"it has been said that on occasion the actors die."

My head jerked up. The waitress stood at our table staring at us curiously. We three looked at her guiltily.

"Sorry it took so long to get back to you fellas, but a girl's got to have a break, you know? Can I get you boys something?" Her gum popped. She scratched inside her beehive hairdo with the tip of her pencil.

We ordered coffee. When I was sure she was out of earshot I whispered, "Snuff movies? Are you sure?"

"No."

"How can he get away with it?" Scott asked.

"If he's doing it, and if he's getting away with it with the complicity of the police and/or politicians, you're dead meat if you get near it. If the police don't know, then he'll be even more vicious in snuffing you out to protect himself."

"Where does all this happen?" I asked.

"I've gone this far," Neil muttered. "You'll find out anyhow. You'll go there. I'm probably signing your death warrant. I hope you find the place empty and deserted."

He told us the address. It was a warehouse on Diversy Avenue, near, I guessed, to where it crossed the North Branch of the Chicago River.

We hurried to the car. Silently Scott drove down Halsted to Diversy and turned west.

"No arguments or objections?" I asked quietly.

"We're going to bust up that motherfucker," he vowed. "It'll be the two of us."

"I'm glad you have such faith in our prowess."

"They won't be expecting us."

"They may not be there at all."

He slammed his fist on the steering wheel. "How could those bastards be killing kids?"

I had no answer to that. I said, "Even if it's deserted we may find some clue that will lead us to Phil." We crossed Lincoln Avenue. "Remember, it was only a rumor," I said.

"Do you doubt it?"

"I find it hard to believe. When Neil thinks the worst about someone, he can go overboard. I'm glad you're willing to go tonight. I'd have walked by myself if you hadn't."

"I know," he said.

We rode in silence. I yawned, whether from nerves or being tired, I couldn't tell. Probably both. In the dashboard light I saw the grim set to Scott's features.

In minutes we were there. First we drove slowly around the building. It was a vast rambling place, a city block wide. The front facing Diversy was all art deco, the sides and back a dull yellow brick interrupted by squares of former windows totally boarded up from inside. No light shone from the warehouse interior. There were no cars parked outside. No one was on the street. The front entrance was deeply recessed and unlit. Dark shadows hid the door, but rather than risk being seen in the lights of a passing car we opted for a rear entrance. Scott drove into an alley across from the back of the warehouse.

He parked in the deepest shadows. The old factories around us were all dark. To our left was the river. We couldn't see it, but its faint acrid reek let us know it was there.

We paused at the curb under the shadow of a lone oak tree. The faint lights from the side streets wouldn't betray our presence anywhere back here. I didn't realize until much later, but for the next hour we spoke in nothing but whispers.

"This is breaking and entering, real criminal offenses," I said.

"Do we have a choice if the kid's in there?" Scott asked.

"No, I don't think so. Calling the police would bring unnecessary delays. North might have clout enough to keep anyone from ever getting inside."

He nodded agreement. We looked at each other a moment. We'd been through a lot, but this was new, dangerous, and illegal. We grinned at each other.

Broken glass gritted under our shoes as we crossed the street and stole across the parking lot.

I pointed to the locks on the door. "Now what? Plus they've got to have a formidable security system."

"No problem," Scott said. He sprinted back to the car. Moments later the soft click of the trunk closing penetrated the night air. I watched him dart back. He brought a tool kit and a flashlight with him. In the dimness he examined the back of the building. Finally he gave me a reassuring smile. "It's a good system, but I can break through. I've installed more complicated ones. All I have to do is—"

I interrupted, "Don't explain. Just do it."

"Okay." He shrugged. "You'll have to boost me onto the roof."

More eternities than I ever want to spend passed as I waited for his return. The occasional rumble of trucks on Diversy Avenue seeped to the back of the warehouse. In the silence my breathing seemed louder than a symphony orchestra. Where was he? I glanced from door to roof and back countless times. After ten minutes I expected alarms to begin screeching any second.

Slowly the door began to open. Your heart really does stop at heart-stopping moments.

Scott poked his head around the opening. "Come on," he urged. "The alarm's off. I broke through a skylight."

Squaring my shoulders, I entered the building. If there was a silent alarm too, there was no hope for us. We shut the door. The area we were in was completely dark. I let my eyes adjust. A few stray beams of light oozed around corners and through chinks in the boards that covered the windows.

It wasn't much, but enough to see we were in a deserted area that ran the length of the back of the building. Double-locked storage bins loomed opposite from us. They stretched to the distance in both directions. Nothing moved in the vast emptiness, not even the rustle of a rat.

"I haven't seen anyone," Scott said. He turned on the flashlight. Quickly he reset the locks on the back door. Uncertain if our light could be seen from outside, we moved quickly to a normal-sized door opposite.

The room we entered was an office with a phone, desk, and filing cabinets. It was windowless. I felt comfortable panning the flashlight around the room. Rapidly we looked through all the drawers for any hint of a clue. A brief search turned up a few paper clips and three crumpled invoices from 1965.

We followed the flashlight through the room's other door. We found ourselves walking through a series of deserted stage settings. Three-quarters of the building must have been devoted to filming. Cameras and lights cluttered most of the areas. We stepped carefully around them. We made little noise. For the moment we were lucky amateurs. Each of the areas had a different motif: one a simple bedroom, one a prison cell, another a nineteenth-century bordello. There were numerous others. We entered a dungeon setting. I went up to the rack.

I motioned Scott over. "Look," I pointed. Splashed on various parts of the rack was blood. "It looks fresh," I said.

A harsh clattering noise froze us in our tracks.

Quickly I doused the light.

I reached out for Scott, found him, and drew him close. I put my lips next to his ear. "Which direction did that come from?"

He shook his head. "I couldn't tell."

We waited for the noise to recur. One light-year passed, then another. I tried to breathe easier. I turned to whisper to Scott. The noise came again louder.

"That's breaking glass," I said into his ear. "Someone else wants to get in."

Above us, this section of the warehouse was two stories high. A grid of steel beams and catwalks crossed the area above. They were backlit by dust-encrusted and begrimed skylights. The lighting was uncertain, but there was enough so that without the flashlight we could make out vague shapes. We moved carefully forward until we could look around the torture rack.

The noise didn't come again. Soon we heard footsteps moving unsteadily about. There was a bang, a series of crashes, and a thump. It sounded like someone ran into one of the cameras or light fixtures, knocking one over and causing a chain reaction. The person swore.

A five-minute silence ensued. My leg muscles began complaining about being forced to remain in one position.

Then a slow scraping sound came from our left. Interminable increments of time crept by as the scraping came closer. Slowly the volume of the scraping increased. Soon I knew the person making the noise was in the same staging area.

I guessed whoever it was didn't belong here as much as we. The person must be equally as frightened. I decided to risk a light.

The second after I pushed the nob the thought struck me—what if this person has a gun? The light would give them an excellent target.

Before I could turn it off, Scott, his eyes quicker to adjust, said, "It's Greg."

It was. We got up stiffly from our hiding place and hurried over to him.

"What the hell are you doing here?" Scott demanded.

"I'm hurt." Greg clutched his left knee.

I pulled the pants leg up. "What happened?" I asked.

"I fell and twisted my knee. Then this big thing dumped square onto it. My knee hurts."

I shined the light on the knee.

The skin wasn't broken. Scott stooped down. Carefully he placed his fingertips on the front, back, and side of the knee. At one point Greg cried out and clinched in agony.

Scott said, "I've seen this kind of thing once before. A guy mashed his knee falling into the dugout while chasing a foul ball. A fifty-pound bag of bats tipped onto his knee as he landed. We have to get you to a doctor. We'll have to carry him."

I nodded. Greg lay on the ground his good leg bent. He was in obvious pain.

"What are you doing here?" I repeated Scott's question.

"Looking for Phil," he said through gritted teeth.

"You knew he was here?" Scott forgot to whisper.

Greg winced in pain. He said, "Not when you left my sister's. I'm not even sure now."

"How'd you find out about this place?"

"I asked my sister more questions when she got back. This is where she said to look. Sometimes kids stayed here, she said, kids who had parts in the movies with no place else to go."

"We haven't found anyone else here, but we've only been through half of it. With all your noise if anybody was here, they've been long since alerted," I said.

"Maybe not, this area is fairly soundproof around stage sets."

"You've been here before."

In the flashlight glow I saw him hang his head. "Yeah, I've been in some of the movies. But I swear, Mr. Mason, I never knew kids stayed here. I never knew they made gay movies either. My sister got me occasional jobs here." He added hurriedly, "In straight porno only."

"Why, Greg?" I asked.

"It was fun. I was popular here. There were no tests like in school. I had one of the major qualifications, my dick could stay hard for hours. Here no one laughed and made fun of my being stupid. It paid decent money too."

Scott asked, "If you were in porno movies, why did it bother you that your sister was a whore?"

"This is a hobby, fun, not a job. I'm not a prostitute. Besides, she's my sister. I have to look out for her." Whether this was misguided sexist chivalry or what I didn't know.

He shifted his weight. The movement made him cry out again. He asked, "How'd you guys find out about this place?"

I told him, leaving out Neil's name. When done explaining I said, "We've searched about half this place. We'll leave you here and finish looking. If Phil is here, he may be tied up, unable to yell. There can't be any guard. They'd be here by now. We'll go as quickly as we can. Then we'll get you to a doctor."

It took fifteen nerve-wracking minutes to go through the rest of the warehouse. Less afraid of noise now, we searched more quickly. There was no sign of Phil. No way of telling if he'd ever been there. The warehouse was a deserted dead end.

We went back for Greg.

"He needs an ambulance," Scott said.

"We can't call. None of us is supposed to be in here," I replied. "Let's get out first. Then we can make decisions."

By clasping each other's arms halfway to the elbow we made a sort of seat for Greg. He handled the tool kit and flashlight and guided us as we moved slowly and awkwardly toward the back. Careful as we were, unfortunate jostlings caused him pain. While Greg wasn't a big person, he was heavy enough that we were forced to stop several times.

At one stop I asked Greg why he hadn't been afraid of tripping the alarm. He shrugged at me. He hadn't thought of it—a naive suburban kid.

I tried to hurry us along. Ten feet from the back exit we had to stop again.

"I'll get the car," Scott said. "We won't have to carry him as far."

I nodded, rubbed my arms to restore the circulation. "Hurry," I called to him, "I want to try the locks on these storage bays before we leave."

"Oh, shit," Scott said from the doorway.

"What?" I asked.

"Someone's coming. There's a moving van backing up in the parking lot."

Scott relocked the door and scrambled over to us. We picked up Greg. He clenched his teeth to stifle his cries of pain. Our haste precluded gentleness.

We hurried through the first door we'd gone through—into the office room. We laid Greg behind the large desk. Scott and I crept back to the door. We opened it a crack and looked out. One of the large garage doors rumbled open. Someone backed up a semi-trailer to the delivery bay. One preson was in the warehouse guiding the truck in. Red lights flashed as the brakes were pumped on and off. We heard a minor thump. The truck lights went out. Darkness returned for a moment. Then the man inside turned a switch. Several bare bulbs poked the darkness with feeble light. Three other men joined the first one.

When the lights came on I thought of closing the door, but it was too late. I was afraid any sudden movement would draw attention to our position.

The four of them began walking toward the door behind which we crouched. They moved casually and at ease. Their errand was not an urgent one, I guessed.

They came closer. Fighting it out with them was absurd. We had Greg to think of so we couldn't try a mad dash to freedom. They got closer—twenty feet, ten feet. Up close I recognized them. All four were at the party earlier. One was Edgar. I could hear their conversation.

One I didn't know said, "I don't see why we have to move this stuff now. I could be in bed with that cute young thing."

"Put a lid on it," another said. "The boss wants this moved now, so now is when we move it."

They were close enough for me to touch them. I held my breath. They walked past the door.

Their voices receded as they passed beyond my line of sight.

I drew a trembling breath. A short time later they returned from some distant storage area carrying large wooden crates. From their stooped posture as they carried the boxes I guessed what was inside must be heavy. They deposited the boxes in the truck and marched back out of our sight.

"We've got to do something," Scott whispered. "They could walk in here any minute."

"I'm open to suggestions," I said.

We were silent as the four of them trudged by with another consignment. After they passed back the other way Scott said, "Why the hell do they have such a huge moving truck? You could put several housefuls of furniture in that one easy."

I said, "Whatever they're up to has to be illegal or why do it at this hour of the morning?"

"I'm going to set off the fire alarm," Scott announced.

"Are you nuts? We're still the illegal ones here."

"While they're distracted with the firemen we grab Greg and clear out. The noise from the alarm will cover our exit."

He moved off before I could grab him and stop him. Seconds later the alarm began clanging. We snatched Greg and headed out toward the front, but it was useless. We made it to the second stage set, and they were right behind us. We hid behind a fake fireplace.

Again we could hear their voices. Edgar definitely was in charge. His authoritative voice, no longer slurred with drink, cut across the distance clearly. "We'll meet them outside," he barked. "We don't want them snooping in here." They all hurried past us toward the front.

"Out the back," I said.

With Greg we made a slow dash to the back entrance. For the first time I saw the open bay they'd been working from. I could make out a ten-foot-high, ten-foot-wide opening filled with the wooden boxes.

When we got to the car I said, "Stay here with Greg. I'm going back to look in that storage bay." I left before Scott could object.

I ran to the warehouse, through the door, and to the storage bay. Quickly I examined the boxes. I tried opening some of them. They'd been nailed tightly shut. The outsides gave no indication of the contents. An aisle between boxes led into the interior. I pushed farther into the room.

I heard footsteps rush up behind me and whirled. It was Scott.

"Hurry," he commanded, looking over his shoulder. "They'll be here any second."

"A minute more." I pushed farther in. I turned a corner. My stomach did a flip. In the dark recesses sat a cramped and grimy movie set. On the floor there was a long box separated from the others. No boxes rested on top of it, because a body dangled there, its toes resting lightly on the lid of the box below. I knew this was where they made the snuff movies.

I rushed to the body. "Scott," I called as loudly as I dared. In a moment he was beside me. His face drained to sickly white.

The body dangled by a short rope tied by the wrists to a beam above. There were deep gash marks on the face and ugly stab wounds on the arms and legs. Up close the body stank, but it was warm to the touch. I saw the chest shudder feebly. "He's alive," I said. We scrambled to untie the knots.

We stood on the box to get to the rope. We had no knife. Precious moments ticked by as we worked at the tangle of knots. We lowered the body. The face was horribly torn and bruised. It was Phil. He was unconscious.

We had him nearly down when Scott stumbled. He fell heavily, smashing open the box beneath. The noise was horrendous. I hoped Edgar and the crew were far away, or that a fireman was nearby and would come to investigate. Anything but Edgar and the boys by themselves.

I'd managed to keep myself and Phil from falling when Scott fell. He picked himself up. I eased Phil to the ground and looked at the newly opened box.

Styrofoam packing material had flown all over. Scott was closer to the box. He turned his head to see what he'd landed in. Then I caught a glimpse.

It was a body. A naked woman—a girl, I corrected after a closer look. She might have been fourteen or fifteen, maybe pretty at one time. She was dead. They had mutilated her worse than Phil, one breast hanging half off.

I listened to Scott being sick in the corner.

I stood up. Inured as I was at one time to death, this was tough. I felt lightheaded, but I kept my stomach under control. We had to get out.

I checked Phil. He breathed shallowly but was otherwise frighteningly still.

"Who's in there?" a harsh voice called from the front.

I walked back down the aisle between the boxes.

Edgar and his cronies blocked the entrance. Edgar had a gun. There was no fireman. For the first time I lost hope.

"One last thing," a voice from behind them called. An immense figure appeared in the opening. His fireman's coat could not hide a figure of some heft. His face bulged redly, topped by a glowing red nose. His ears stuck out from under his fireman's hat. He was uglier than a mud fence. I could have kissed him. Other firemen crowded behind him. None of them could see the gun.

"These men are murderers," I announced loudly.

"This man is here illegally. He must have broken in," Edgar said. "I want you to arrest him—them," he corrected as Scott walked up beside me. Scott wobbled as he walked, barely recovered.

I talked directly to the firemen. "There's a dead body back there and a boy who needs immediate medical attention—if it isn't already too late."

The situation was one Edgar hadn't prepared for. He couldn't kill all of us, or murder me in front of such a crowd. He swung the gun to cover the whole group.

The fat, ugly fireman caught the movement. His hand blurred and the gun skittered across the floor.

"Run," Edgar yelled. He and the boys made a break for it. The big fireman moved faster than an all-pro lineman. He blocked three of them, but Edgar sprinted around him and then through the other startled firemen. I gave chase. He got halfway to the truck only because I had to leap over several boxes before I hit full stride. I tackled him elegantly. There was a delightful crack as his skull met the pavement. He didn't move.

They called ambulances to take Phil and Greg. I asked to go with them, but the police wanted us there for questioning.

It was long past dawn when we finished talking to the cops. I gulped coffee to stay awake. Scott, quiet through most of the interrogation, added nods of confirmation at critical points. Cops appeared in the background to stare at him. No one asked for an autograph.

Kiddie porn filled the boxes ready for shipment to distributors.

The police arrested Edgar and the other three. I never did get their names. The police led them away to waiting police cars.

We wound up at the 18th district police station on Chicago Avenue.

Around seven I called school to say I wouldn't be in.

At nine-fifteen Frank Murphy and John Robertson showed up.

Robertson wore a scowl, but stayed silent for most of the conversation. Frank seemed to be in charge for the moment.

The Chicago cop who'd been questioning us, Lieutenant King, greeted Frank by his first name. They obviously knew each other.

King told them the story. "We owe these two a pretty big vote of thanks," he concluded.

Frank smiled as he said, "Yeah, they wouldn't listen to us and keep their noses clean."

I wasn't in the mood for anybody's smile. "Did we uncover a major criminal operation? A dead kid?" I asked.

"Yeah," Frank said, "take it easy."

"Sorry, I'm tired," I apologized. I turned to King. "Who was the girl?"

"We don't know," he answered.

"Could the medical people tell what happened?" I asked.

"Only the obvious for now—someone tortured both kids for an extended period. She probably died from the wounds. We won't know for sure until she's been examined at the lab."

"It might be on a film," I said.

"We'll go through all of them, of course. Everything there will be inspected carefully," the lieutenant said.

"Will you arrest North?" I asked.

"We'll question him, but right now we have those four guys." He flipped his notebook shut. "You two can go after you sign a statement. By the way, the commander told us to overlook your little break-in."

"Thanks," we both muttered.

"No problem. The department can't arrest the city's biggest baseball hero after he breaks up a kiddie-porn ring and discovers a murder. Speaking of which, the press has been crawling around. Word is out you're here, Mr. Carpenter. If you want when you're done, we can get you out of here without you having to mess with them."

"Thanks," Scott said.

To the two suburban cops King said, "I imagine you'll want to talk to them." He left.

Frank sat on the edge of a cluttered desk. Robertson stood by the door. Scott sat on a black cotlike couch next to the desk. I slouched in the chair behind the desk.

"Did these guys kill Evans?" Scott asked.

"Yes," Robertson said.

"No," I said.

We glared at each other. He looked away first.

"Let me tell you what we found in the last thirty-six hours," I said.

I told them everything. They wrote busily as I spoke. At one point Frank placed a call to the station giving them the access code to the disc. I felt a twinge of guilt in breaking my promise to Sylvester and Armstrong when I told him the code. But the explanation made no sense without it. Still, I didn't reveal the significance of the data to them. At least they'd have to figure that out by themselves.

I finished my explanation.

"Lock them both up," Robertson snarled when I finished.

Frank grinned at him. "I don't think so. The press will make a deal out of this. You heard King. They'll play the Carpenter hero angle big. Do you really want to be the one responsible for arresting the hero of the hour? And remember, at the moment we have no jurisdiction or standing here."

"How did you two know about all this?" I asked.

"Courtesy call," Frank answered. "When you talked so much about what happened to Evans, the lieutenant called me."

"I got the impression he knew you."

"We grew up in Chicago in the same neighborhood. We were in the same class in the training academy. I moved to the suburbs. He stayed in the city." Frank shifted his weight on the desk, "Back to the subject at hand. Why didn't these guys kill Evans?"

"Evans wasn't a threat to their boss. Nowhere on the data disc did it indicate anything that would link him to North."

"Maybe you didn't recognize it," Frank said.

"I'm pretty sure I would have. Once you understand how he tracked the data, it's pretty easy to follow."

"Okay. North wasn't on the disc. Go ahead."

"North wouldn't have him killed. Remember, they were working a deal that last night. No, the scheme with North was a constant supply of vast sums of ready cash for both of them. Evans gambled his away. Then he borrowed from North. Evans always needed more. He turned to all the ways I've described to make it."

"Then Vance could still be our man," Robertson said.

"No, don't forget, the administrator saw Evans alive later."

"So he's our man?"

"I can't see it. I admit I've been suspicious of them, and I don't trust them, but administrators are a generic lot. As a rule they wouldn't have the courage to kill someone. This guy is the same."

"From what you've said he doesn't have an alibi."

"No, but I just don't think he did it. And according to North, his man Edgar saw Evans even later than Armstrong." I admitted feeling odd defending an administrator.

Robertson snapped, "We'll be questioning him."

More calmly Frank said, "We'll be requestioning everybody. We'll have to puzzle it out."

"Are you going to go deeper into this set-up here?" I inquired.

"No," Frank answered, "This was a separate matter. This was a source of money, not murder in my opinion. This isn't our problem. We need to solve a simple suburban murder."

"Are you going to release Vance?" I asked.

"I imagine so," Frank said. He eased himself off the desk. They went off to requestion suspects and witnesses. We went to Scott's to get some sleep.

We woke up at three in the afternoon. I called the hospital. Greg had been released. They wouldn't tell us much about Phil. I called Greg's house. Other than a broken knee, he was fine.

Before we went to see Phil in the hospital I called Frank Murphy to see if Vance had been released. When Frank said yes, I called Vance at home. We stopped at his house before we went to the hospital.

He greeted us effusively. "I owe you both a great deal. The police told me what you did. I can't thank you enough."

I asked him to explain the gambling operation to us in light of what we found on the disc.

He said, "It started small, just a few of us. We went on that way for a long time. For a while it simply grew. Then one day we woke up and it was too big for us."

"Too big? How so?"

"Two ways. One, on big events we had to cover too many bets. Soon we wouldn't be able to afford our own success. That led to the second problem. We made too much money. The local bookmaking people were unhappy. That's where we made our mistake. Evans said he knew someone who could solve our problem. I didn't want to trust Evans, but there wasn't much choice. In an amazingly short time Evans was in full control."

"How did he keep control?"

"He knew an enforcer who could collect from people who wouldn't pay. When we were small no one cared if someone owed. We carried them until they could pay. With Evans, if people got behind the enforcer came for a visit."

"How about yourself? You owed a great deal."

"I was paying in installments. A lot of the money Evans had on him that night was mine."

"I understand," I said. "Do you know how Evans lost so much money?"

"That I don't know. I presume he gambled heavily and lost."

"It's that simple, I guess," I said.

When we got up to leave I asked him why he told Armstrong about my visits.

"Sylvester followed you to my office. I couldn't deny it. Armstrong threatened me. I'm afraid I'm not a strong man."

We went to the hospital to see Phil. Mrs. Evans and Keith were there along with Heather Delacroix. They formed a group around a doctor outside Phil's room. We hurried to join them. After introducing ourselves to the doctor, we asked how Phil was.

"I just told Mrs. Evans that external injuries aren't bad. We've talked to a plastic surgeon already. He assures us that in time Phil can look normal again." She shook her head. "It's his internal injuries we have to worry about right now. We're still testing to find the extent of the damage. The beating he took is worse than any I've seen in my fifteen years of practice. As soon as I get the final results later this afternoon I'll be in to tell you more."

Mrs. Evans leaned heavily against Heather. The social worker led her to a bench. "Did you want to ask the doctor any questions?" Heather asked.

Mrs. Evans shook her head a feeble no.

"Perhaps I could get something for Mrs. Evans?" the doctor said.

Mrs. Evans took out a handkerchief from her purse and began twisting it in her hands. She'd dart quick dabs at her eyes and nose with it, then go back to mauling the hanky. Heather answered for her. "Why don't you bring something, Doctor? I'll see if I can't get her to take it."

"Can we see Phil?" I asked before the doctor left.

She looked us over carefully. Heather, who'd obviously talked with the doctor before, nodded and spoke up for us. The doctor let us in.

We entered the room. Keith slipped in with us. He hadn't said anything, simply stood mutely watching the circle of adults in the hushed presence of familial tragedy. He wore a jeans jacket over a Chicago Bears sweatshirt.

Keith stood between us as we placed ourselves at the side of Phil's bed. He was awake. Thick bandages covered his face and arms. He smiled when his eyes lit on Keith. Phil held out his hand to his younger brother. Awkwardly, uncertainly, the thirteen-year-old took it.

"How are you, tiger?" Phil's voice came out a hoarse croak.

"I'm okay," Keith whispered back.

"I wish they'd let you see me earlier."

"They wouldn't let me."

"That's okay. You're here now."

He occasionally rasped for extra breath. He lay unnaturally still. His head inclined only slightly toward us. His eyes blinked, and his hand clutched Keith's—no other movement.

"Thanks for rescuing me, you guys," he said to us. "The police have asked me as many questions as the doctor would allow. They told me you found me."

"How did you wind up there?"

His eyes shut briefly before he started his story. "I tried to leave North's stable. I found out he and my dad worked together."

"How did you find out?"

"I overheard two of his assistants talking about somebody named Evans. At first I thought it was me they were talking about, but some of what they said didn't make sense. Then it dawned on me that they were talking about my dad. Later I talked to one of the guys I trusted. He filled me in. He was surprised I didn't know. I confronted North. He laughed at my ignorance. I didn't want to stay. I didn't want anything to do with somebody connected to a slime like my dad. I walked out on North. He warned me not to. He said I'd be sorry. I escaped. I ran straight to Daphne."

A slight laugh escaped his lips. "She delayed me in the bar long enough to call North and have two of the gang come get me. I tried to get a message to Greg, but he came in only five minutes before the goon squad showed up. I only had time to tell him to call for help."

"Greg knew about the Womb?" I asked.

"Yeah. The cops told me about him being with you guys. He used to come to the Womb once in a while. He wasn't gay or anything. Sometimes the cast and crew from a movie would go there to celebrate after they wrapped it up. They added a little more sleaze, as if you'd notice in that place."

"He must have been the one who called your mom." I explained my guess to Phil.

"It must have been him. She was the wrong person to call."

"He did his best," I said.

"Yeah, he never was the brightest, but a good guy."

"So what happened?" I asked.

"They took me to the warehouse. I managed to get to a phone and call Keith. Your number isn't listed, Mr. Mason. I tried to get you first. That's why I didn't have much time to talk to Keith, but I knew I could count on him to get you."

For a moment Phil's hand squeezed Keith's more tightly.

"They caught me before I could say much. It was worse after that. They tied me up, tortured me." He stopped for a while. As he talked he'd occasionally pause in obvious pain. In a few minutes he collected himself and continued. "After that I don't remember much until I woke up here."

Phil turned his attention to Keith, drawing the youngster closer. "If anything happens to me, if I die—"

"You're not going to die," Keith interrupted.

"You've got to listen, tiger. Please, cool down like the other night. Remember what I said that night. I promised no one would ever hurt you again."

Keith nodded.

"I meant it. No one is ever going to bother you, ever. That's what's going to make me better, my promise to you." His breathing came shallow and uneven. The emotional exertion drained him.

"Take it easy, Phil," I warned.

He ignored me. "Keith, I want you to promise me now though. If I don't get better, you will be strong and take care of yourself. I got away. You can too. You know we both broke away once." He gasped heavily.

Keith shook his head. "You're not going to die. You can't."

Phil lay back completely drained. His face turned stark white. His features clenched in agony. I summoned the nurse. She bustled us out of the room. Minutes later the doctor hurried by us into the room.

Heather met us outside, "Mrs. Evans is under sedation. I've got her napping down the hall."

Then all hell broke loose. People began rushing in and out of Phil's room. They flung large machines through the door. An hour passed. We couldn't get any answers to our questions.

The doctor came out. She came over to us. "Where is Mrs. Evans?" she asked.

Heather explained.

"Better get her," the doctor said. She looked at the rest of us. "It won't hurt if you all come in now."

"How is he?" I asked.

She shook her head.

We entered the room. People and machines surrounded the bed. We stayed in the background. Keith craned his neck trying to see his brother over and around the machines.

Mrs. Evans came in led by Heather. They made room for her on one side of Phil's bed. She took his hand. I leaned down and whispered that it was all right for Keith to go to his brother if he wanted.

He gave a violent shake of his head. His eyes were saucer wide with fear.

Phil was dead. The nurses and doctors left one by one dragging their machines behind them. The original doctor said a few low words of comfort to Mrs. Evans, then stopped where we were.

I explained to her what happened at the end with Phil and Keith. She caught on quickly. She said to Keith, "You are never to think that you had any part in Phil's death. You're what kept him alive, I suspect. He held on so he could talk to you. His internal injuries were massive, beyond anybody's ability to cure. He died for medical reasons, not because he talked to you."

Keith seemed to understand, but he said nothing. He moved closer to us. The doctor looked at us and said, "Take care of him." We said we would. She left.

Mrs. Evans stared at her son. She barely moved. Heather murmured to her. Mrs. Evans moved closer and touched Phil's hand, then his face. She lingered in silence. Eventually Heather led Mrs. Evans away. I began to move to follow, but Keith remained rooted in place. I went back to him.

Keith stared at the bed.

I put my hand on his shoulder. "We have to go now," I whispered. Again he shook his head violently no. He brushed my hand off.

"I'm sorry, Keith, I wish we could have saved him sooner. We can stay here a little longer, but then we'll have to go."

He stared at the bed. "He was the best brother in the whole world." His words came out small and frightened. "He always protected me. I was never a pest to him. He took me places when I was little—to ball games, and the zoo, and the beach, and every Sunday afternoon in our old neighborhood we walked together the three blocks to the old movie theater. We'd sit through each show twice. I want him back."

I knew I had to ask the question. I wanted to keep it to myself forever. I was afraid of the answer. I said, "Keith, what did Phil mean when he said that about 'breaking away' and 'cooling down like the other night'?"

He continued to stare at his brother.

I asked softly, "What happened the other night?"

Scott gave me a sharp look, as if to say go easy on the kid. Keith didn't see it.

"I killed him," Keith said. "He got me up out of bed. It was real late. He made me get dressed. He said he had someone he wanted me to meet. I asked a bunch of questions, but he wouldn't answer. But Phil had warned me. He said if Dad attacked me or acted suspicious, to come get him, and that if he wasn't around to run as far and fast as I could and that Phil would come protect me or find me.

"My dad and me were in the garage. I told him I wouldn't go, that I wanted Phil. He knocked me down. We wrestled. He was too big. He threw me down. He tried to push me into the car. I got away. I screamed at him to stop. I grabbed the nearest thing, my baseball bat. I yelled for Phil. He'd gone out around eleven o'clock. I didn't know if he was home. When I yelled my dad got madder. He came at me like he was crazy. I dodged and ran outside. He came at me on the lawn. He was too big to run away from. I swung the bat with all my might. I hit him. He fell. He made a lot of noise. I kept hitting him over and over and screaming. I think my mom heard, but she never came. My dad was dead. As I stood over him Phil drove up.

"Phil said they'd never believe a little kid's story. And things would only be worse for me if anyone found out. We had to get him out of there. We put the body in the backseat of the car. Phil helped me straighten up the garage."

I remembered Phil's story about the rain that night. Any evidence in the grass would have been washed away.

"Why'd you pick my classroom to put him in?"

"We wanted to put him in his own classroom. Phil knew my dad was involved in lots of illegal stuff at work. He said everybody would figure it was something to do with that.

"Getting into school was pretty easy, but his body was heavy. It was around five o'clock, and the first janitors showed up just as we got in the door by your room. We couldn't carry him back out. They could see us. We decided to put him in the nearest room and get out while we could.

"Phil knew how to open all the doors in the school. He and his friends had broken in a couple times years ago. We put him in a desk far back so he couldn't be seen from the window. No one saw us leave. Phil drove my dad's car to a side street in Chicago. I followed him in his car. He let me drive it sometimes, so I knew how. We drove back in plenty of time. We went to school like regular." He paused. He walked over to the bed, smoothed the already perfect cover. He looked back over his shoulder at us.

"I think my mom guessed the truth," he said, "that's why she's been so bad lately."

He stopped smoothing the bed. His hands rested at his sides, his head drooped forward. I walked to him, put my hand on his shoulder. He didn't brush it away this time.

I let the silence build. I felt the anger that had built up inside him, and now the added sorrow of his brother's death. Tears started down his face. All his hatreds, loneliness, fears, and living nightmares broke out, and he wept.

I put my arms around him and held him tightly. He buried his tears in my shirtfront. None of us it seems has enough magic to protect the children.

10

I sat on the couch in my living room gazing out the picture window at the sunset. Hours before Scott ordered me out of the kitchen. It was Thanksgiving. Cooking noises drifted sporadically to my ears. I smiled at the sunset. I felt peaceful and rested—the kind of moment you remember from childhood when you were completely safe, which you wish you could replicate as an adult and then keep forever. But it's only a memory and a fleeting pang of calm and regret.

Two weeks had passed since we solved the murder. We'd talked until dawn that next morning. Neither of us disagreed, but we had to be sure. We didn't turn Keith in. He wasn't a criminal. He'd acted in self-defense. He didn't need to be crushed by an unfeeling bureaucracy. What the juvenile justice system could do to a kid was worse than many crimes. What his family had done to him was enough horror for one lifetime. We'd visited him several times. Heather Delacroix promised she would remain close to the family situation as long as necessary.

From Frank we'd learned that Evans had been offered $10,000 for Keith for a weekend. He was to bring Keith to meet Edgar and the group that night for them to see the boy for final approval. Frank confirmed that Evans was desperate for money and greedy as hell.

We attended Phil's funeral. Scott and I talked for hours that night agonizing about whether or not we could have saved Phil if we'd acted differently. Finally Scott said that there's a lot of what ifs in this world. He gave examples. What if we'd tested positive for the AIDS antibodies? We didn't. We're among the lucky ones. What if you get hit by a car tomorrow? You can "what if" yourself forever. He told me to forget it and concentrate on the now.

I'm not the type for regrets, and Scott was right.

The cops acted like they had been acting. Robertson was an asshole and still wanted to arrest us for his own obscure reasons. Frank thanked us. He told me he'd keep in touch. Through him I found out about the North case. So far he had been questioned but not arrested. The cops shut down the porno operation, of course. They arrested three more people connected with it. They hadn't found out how Evans and North had originally connected. I'm not sure it mattered anymore. The dead girl was still unidentified. To me that was one of the saddest things about the whole case. Who were her mom and dad? Where were they? Were their hearts breaking somewhere, or did they even care? Frank said the possibilities of tracing her were small.

Getting a murder conviction in Phil's and her case might prove difficult. Expensive lawyers hired by North played the system. We closed down one lethal porno operation. Convictions and closing others was somebody else's business.

Meg had called early this morning. Rumors had run rampant around school for two weeks about major changes coming.

The local paper, which came out twice a week—Sundays and Thursdays—had the announcement this morning. I wanted to pick up a copy later. Meg told us that at last night's school board meeting Sylvester and Armstrong resigned. The paper didn't give the details she said, although it did say the board accepted the resignations with regrets. Criminal prosecution wasn't mentioned. I wasn't sure I cared about that now.

Of course reporters got hold of the story. Star player, hero catches crooks. It made the national news. The police helped a great deal to keep that kind of chaos to a minimum. The ball club's publicity spokesperson, Sylvia Finsterwald, did an excellent job. She was fifty-six years old, gray haired, and efficient as hell. I think she liked me. I hope she did. She kept the interviews and harassment to a mild uproar the first few days and to a bare minimum after that. Scott did most of the interviews. He does them all summer and half the winter anyway. He's good at it. Plus the sports writers love him because he gives interviews readily. He wanted me to get more publicity. I convinced him I really wasn't interested.

I got off the couch and walked to the window. It was my favorite time of the day. The last blues and grays hung suspended in the sky. Darkness gathered around the edges of all the bushes and trees that sloped to the distant fields. A star or two twinkled in a cloudless sky.

Scott walked up behind and put his arms around me. He rested his head on my shoulder. I felt his chest against my back.

"Dinner will be ready in fifteen minutes," he whispered.

Years ago we decided Thanksgiving was our own. A kind of anniversary celebration for ourselves, I guess. He cooks the meal. I did the first year. We wound up at the only McDonalds in fifty miles open on Thanksgiving. Since then he cooks. He's not half bad.

"How are you feeling?" he asked.

"Content," I said.

"You know"—he hesitated, then plunged on. "While I made dinner I—" He stopped.

I turned to look at him. His eyes reflected back the deep blue of the fading horizon. I wanted to lose myself in them forever.

Scott said, "I thought about all that's happened to us in these eight years and especially what we went through the past month."

He cleared his throat, but his eyes remained steadily looking into mine. "The most important thing in all that's happened was the—" He stopped again. When he resumed his voice had reached its deepest thrum. "Remember that first night in the bar—the Womb? While you were in the washroom the bartender propositioned me. I turned him down. He asked me why not? I said it was because I love you.

"And you know, I realized I haven't said that to you in a long time." He gazed at me in the last lights of dusk. "So, Tom Mason, I love you. I love you very, very much."

He put his arms around me and held me tight. I melted into his warmth and strength. This was safest of all.